DEAD

AR Schnell

Copyright © 2015 AR Schnell

All rights reserved

ISBN: 151696087

For my parents, for being great editors as well as cheerleaders.

For my friends; Kerry, Ashley, Monica, BreAnn and Al. Your notes made the process worthwhile.

For Ben and his smoking references.

You all made this possible.

Chapter 1

So yeah, I just got stabbed.

It was pretty obvious. I was walking down the street, doing whatever when some guy jumped out and stabbed me in broad daylight. They got me right through the heart too.

I know this probably brings up millions of questions. I have a million too. No, there wasn't any pain. At least I don't think there was pain. I can't remember. I can't remember most of it actually. I just know it happened. I could swear it happened, like knowing about a movie a friend told you about even though you've never seen it yourself.

I also know I passed out. I must have passed out, because I'm lying on my side and I don't remember what happened five seconds ago. The previous event had only dimly registered in my head. That was it. I was stabbed and I blacked out. When woke up— whenever that was— I sat up, ran a hand through my hair and tried to figure out what the hell was going on.

Above me was a blue sky was cut off by various buildings, sky scrapers, etc. Muffled footsteps were barely audible above the sound of cars screeching to a halt. The growing sound of a siren began to register in my dim ears. I realized I must be in some kind of city. How I got here, I didn't really know.

5
Dead

I looked down to find a various people crowding me. I wasn't surprised, considering what happened. Strangers cast looks of concern and astonishment everywhere I turned. Their whispers and voices were drowned out by the siren and other cars. I wasn't in much shock myself. I felt normal. I wasn't in any pain, and my only concern was why this had happened to me.

And why was I walking down the street in the first place? Let's see, I was—

Where was I going? Come to think of it, where had I come from? The most logical explanation was I came from my home.

But where was that?

My hand came up to my chest. I tried to remember my past. I frowned. I tried to remember my friends, my family, anything that ever happened in my life. I couldn't. My fingers slowly curled around the fabric of my shirt. The memories wouldn't come. My brain felt like a blank piece of paper, like a whole chunk of my mind was missing. I didn't know what happened five years ago. I didn't know what happened five minutes ago! I didn't know if I was on my way to help someone or running away from a crime scene. I had no idea who I was.

I didn't even know my name.

I looked back to the crowd in front of me. I considered asking them if they knew who I was, or if anyone saw a guy with a knife running around. But they all seemed too shocked to do anything. No one pulled out a phone to call 911 or offered a hand to help me up. They just stood there.

It felt as if the bleeding had stopped in my chest. I held out my shirt, letting out an inward groan at the killer stain on my clothes. I pulled myself up, dusting the dirt off my jeans. It was then I started to really look at the crowd. There was familiar yellow tape holding the people back. Police cars were scattered in the streets, and policemen were directing people through traffic. I might have lost my memory, but I definitely knew what that meant.

Someone had called an ambulance. It was parked in the middle of the road, more yellow tape blocking it from other cars. A path through crowd soon appeared, and from it, some workers were carrying a stretcher towards me.

"Hey wait," I called, holding up my hands. "It's fine. I'm ok, see?"

But the people didn't stop, they were barreling straight toward me. I finally had to jump aside before I ended up on the ground again. As I regained balance, almost stumbled into the building next to me. That's when I saw him.

It was a boy, about sixteen. He was lying on the ground, arms and legs sprawled out on the stained cement. Jet black hair stuck up like a tangle of wires, with a few pieces hanging over his bloody, bruised forehead. His green-gray eyes were wide open, staring into the sky he could no longer see. And in the middle of his chest, cutting through his navy sweatshirt, gushed a ring of blood.

He was dead, definitely dead. Something must have pierced his heart, like a bullet or something.

I replayed that thought: he was *dead*. I was lying on top of a dead body. Staring death in the face so suddenly, I couldn't think straight. My head was spinning, and I felt like I might pass out again. How did this guy get here? Did I fall on top of him? Knock him over?

"Um, excuse me?" I asked, turning back to the people carrying the stretcher. But when I turned I saw they were a few millimeters from running me over. And he they didn't stop. They hit me straight on, knocking me back onto the sidewalk.

I caught myself with my hands before I could kiss the cement. Though my hands scraped against the ground, surprisingly I wasn't hurt. I scrambled out from underneath the stretcher and got back to me feet. They just ran me over. They didn't even pause or anything. What was with these people?

"Hey!" I yelled, running after them. A few feet away I passed the window of a building when something caught my eye. I paused to look—and I froze.

Jet black hair, like tangled wires. A few pieces of hair stuck to a bloody, bruised forehead. There were green grey eyes and a navy sweatshirt.

8
Dead

No. That was impossible. I looked just like—

But that wasn't possible. That guy was on a stretcher, that guy was covered in blood. That guy was dead, and I—

I was still alive, wasn't I? I had somehow survived my accident, and I was still here, right? I mean, I wasn't see-through or flying up to some giant white light or anything. Dead people went to heaven, right? I wasn't dead, that was impossible!

I glanced over to see that they were carrying the stretcher to the ambulance, the body placed on top.

"Wait!" I yelled, dashing after them. None of them looked up. No one could hear me. No, this wasn't happening. No. No. No. No.

I reached the stretcher and gripped the sides with my hands. I couldn't take my eyes away from the body, my body. This wasn't real! I grabbed my corpse by the shoulder and shook it, as if trying to wake it up. But the body wouldn't even move. I couldn't move it. I didn't have muscles anymore.

I tried to reach inside the corpse's chest, trying to see if I could somehow crawl back inside the body and come back to life. But my hand only pounded on the unmoving corpse, as useless as trying to punch through a wall. I got forehead to forehead, nose to nose with my own body, trying with everything I had to push myself back inside.

Dead

With a bump, I was knocked off the stretcher. The corpse was being rolled into the ambulance. Before I could get back to my feet the doors were shut. I charged the ambulance, body slamming into the red doors. I bounced off like a Ping-Pong ball.

It was no use. I straightened up and looked around at the crowd of people. Someone had to be able to see me. *Someone* had to be able to help me.

"Hello?" I shouted, turning away from my body. "Anyone?!" Panic started to rise up inside me. Panic without a heart to race. I ran up to the nearest person, some guy that had carried the stretcher. I waved my hands in front of his face, yelling and shouting at him.

The man didn't even blink. I tried to grab him by the shirt in an attempt to shake him into realizing someone else was here. But I couldn't get a grip. I couldn't move him.

I couldn't move my own body. I couldn't move that man. I couldn't fold the fabric of his clothes into a grip. I always thought ghosts just went through things, that they couldn't move, but this was not the case. My hands just stayed on his shirt, not able to do anything. I couldn't move him, I couldn't go through him.

He kept on walking and ended up knocking me along with him. He would've kept on pushing me too if I hadn't gotten out of the way.

10
Dead

I looked around at the people walking up and down the city streets. All of them were either not paying attention or casting sad looks at the ambulance. Everyone just looked through me. It was like I wasn't even there, like I didn't exist.

"Anyone?" I called again slowly. My nonexistent nerves bounced around inside me. No one looked up, not even the people right next to me.

Honestly, I knew no one would hear me. Not now, not ever. But I had to be wrong. There had to be a way, somehow, I could get someone's attention. Someone had to know what was going on.

"HEEEEEEEEEEEEEEEYYYYYYYY!"

Normally my throat would have started to hurt. But now the only thing that hurt was reality. A hand came up to my throat, feeling the skin on my neck that wasn't really there. I tried to remember how to breathe, how to start panting nervously, how take in and exhale oxygen.

But it wouldn't work. I didn't know who I was, where I was, or where I had come from. But I knew one thing was absolutely certain.

I was dead.

Chapter 2

The ambulance began to pull away. I jerked my head back to the crowd, the police. They couldn't leave me here. I couldn't be left behind. The body, *my* body, was in that car.

"Wait!"

I bolted. The top of my head brushed police tape as I ducked into the crowd. Moments came and past in a singular blur. I was in front of the crowd, in the crowd, behind the crowd, on the street. I was weaving between pedestrians that couldn't see me. I had to get to that ambulance.

My feet were running and my arms were pumping, but it wasn't the same. I wasn't panting. Sweat didn't run down my forehead. There was no swish of my clothes or feeling of wind in my hair. I didn't have any memories of jogging, but I knew it wasn't the same. Running made people feel alive, and I was far from that.

The vehicle was already close to turning the corner. A long wail sounded from its rooftop as it made its way toward the busy road. As fast as I could I charged down the road after my body. It was sometime in late afternoon, so the number of cars was kind of a problem. Even without a body to slow me down, I couldn't keep up with the vehicle as it began to build speed. I couldn't go any faster than a living person.

Dead

I rounded the corner, eyes darting around for my red and white coffin. Although I kept pushing forward, I began to slow down. I didn't have muscles, but I couldn't carry on. It was like something inside me— my core or whatever I was made of— seemed to feel weak with exhaustion.

I finally stopped, an uneasy feeling in my nonexistent gut. The intersection was packed. Tall buildings surrounded busy sidewalks and gave the perfect image of a city you'd see on TV. But nothing looked familiar. I scanned for the source of the long screaming horn, but I had no luck. The ambulance had gone, its wail fading into the distance.

"No," I found myself saying. There was no reason to keep my thoughts quiet. This couldn't happen. I wouldn't let this happen.

I started running again. I ran deeper into the strange new city, following the wailing to the best of my ability. I ran forever, rounding so many corners and so many streets. The city felt like a maze. Only this one had no exit. It felt like my ears were playing tricks on me. One minute I could see the ambulance rounding the corner and the next it sounded miles away from me. It took a good half an hour before I realized it was gone, really gone. It didn't matter which corner I turned or what the sound told me. I couldn't find it again.

I paused in the middle of the street. It seemed like my core-energy-or-whatever was too tired to continue. I had lost my body, and any way of finding it. An uneasy feeling hit me with a pang. My family— I assumed I had a family— would be contacted, and I'd have no way to reach them.

But I was still here. I was still on this earth for some reason. And whoever was out there for me, I could find them.

The wailing was almost gone now. I looked up and scanned the buildings around me. I was definitely in some major city, but I didn't know where. Shops were along either side of the street, steady traffic in the road—

Wham!

The next thing I knew I was on the road face down, the underside of a taxi above me. Like the first time, it didn't hurt, but it was rather inconvenient. Like a flash the vehicle continued on its way and I had to roll away from the oncoming traffic. When I hit the curb I stood up and headed for the sidewalk.

"Hey," I barked at the car, which was almost out of my view. "Watch where you're going!" Like it mattered what I said anymore. "You're gonna kill someone!"

My hands dug into my pockets. I continued down the street, heading towards nowhere. Where did I go from here? Even if I found my body, it wasn't like it could tell me what to do. What was the point?

I found a can lying on the ground and in anger, tried to kick it. But my foot only bounced off. It was like I had kicked a brick wall without the pain. I snarled at the ground.

14
Dead

None of this was right. I couldn't pass through things and I couldn't even move a stupid can. I was dead, but things weren't supposed to be like this.

Come to think of it, why was I dead? I knew how, but *why?* Why would someone come along and stab me, out of all the ways to die? What made me so important? I scoffed, like it mattered anymore.

"Everyone!" I called, voice booming down the street. "Guess what? I'm *dead.*"

People continued to walk by, cars passed. Somewhere in the distance a dog barked. I took a step back and summoned as much strength as I could.

"CAN ANYONE HEAR ME?"

It felt weird yelling like this without having to breathe. I waited. If I'd been alive, I'm pretty sure I would've made an echo. But it wasn't enough. I backed up even more, throwing my head back with one last effort.

"HELLLLOOOOOO?"

"Hey!"

I looked up.

"Shut up," a boy said to me.

I stopped and turned to the speaker. Was that my imagination, or was he talking to me? There were a group

Dead

of kids by a bus stop. They were all dressed in football jerseys and hollering at one another as the bus pulled up. They all seemed like friends, so of course they'd be talking to each other.

The stranger smiled at me. "You should see your face. You look like you've seen a ghost."

From a bench at the bus stop, the guy who'd spoken was smirking at me. He was a few years younger than me, but that didn't matter. He was alive, and he was staring *at me*. He was sitting on top of the back rest, his feet resting on the seat. He wore a yellow and black skater shirt. His red-brown hair stuck out from behind his ears, topped with a red beanie.

"What?" I asked, too surprised to comprehend.

"I said you look pale. Like you've seen a ghost," he repeated, snickering at his own joke, "and you were screaming. It's kind of rude."

I stared at him, wondering whether he was serious or not.

"No offense of course. But seriously, there's like this unsaid rule that you don't scream your head off in public. You might wanna think about it."

I blinked, confused. "Huh?"

"Never mind," the boy swung his feet around to face me. "Who're you looking for?"

"Hold on," I cut in, frowning. "How can you see me right now?"

"You're the one running around talking to yourself," he shrugged with a modest smile. "It draws attention."

"But no one else can see me."

The bus doors closed with the rest of the kids already on board. I had assumed the boy was with this group, but he wasn't moving. I looked from the bus to him, but he didn't seem to notice.

"You're ride is leaving."

"I was just watching. It's not mine."

He wasn't wearing a jersey like the other kids were. He was a tad younger too. The boy remained on the bench, nodding for me to go on.

"Who are you?" I asked. How come this guy could see me? Did this mean he was dead too? He watched me, taking in the bloody mess I probably was.

"You're a weird one," he decided finally. "How'd you get here?"

I debated whether to go through the story of not. "There was an ambulance I need to find. I can't find anything in this city." I stopped there. I didn't need this guy's help.

He spread out his arms and gestured to everything around him. "Welcome to Chicago."

Chicago? I ran the word through my mind, trying to see if any memory was attached.

"Oh, and another thing: it's rude to stare," the boy added, leaning back. "It's kind of creepy, actually."

"I asked who you were," I reminded him. Chicago: the word came up blank. I knew I had to have some memory, some recollection of this place, but nothing came. What was wrong with me?

"Well if you have to know Mr. Pushy, I'm Rowley," he answered. "You're *really* new here aren't you? Is that blood?"

"Yeah," I replied, stepping back. I forgot I was bruised and bloody.

"You look really freaked out," he noted, cocking his head. "I mean, you know you're *dead*, right?"

"I noticed that when they carried off my body," I nodded.

"Well you don't act like it," he commented. "The living people can't see ya, hear ya, or touch ya—with the exception of some mediums, certain children and animals. Everyone knows that."

"Well, I'm new to all this."

"I could tell," he agreed. "The new ones usually run around like that for a few days. What's your name anyway?"

I drew a blank, "I'm—" No words came to mind. No sudden burst of recognition told me who I was, let alone what to say. "That's none of your business."

"Charmed," Rowley replied. "Clyde's gonna wanna see you anyway," he continued, grabbing my hand. "It's not that far from here."

"I'm not going anywhere until I find my body," I interrupted. He had grabbed my hand. He *touched* me. And what's more, I could touch him. That was the most interaction I've had with anyone for as long as I could remember. Technically that wasn't very long, but that's not the point. I wasn't going to let this guy lead me around.

"Your body, need some closure?" he asked. "Sure. Where're ya buried?"

I didn't know what hospital I was taken to, let alone where I'd be buried. "That's none of your business either. I'll find it on my own."

I turned, walking in the opposite direction a little faster than I should.

"Hey, wait! Dead Guy!"

He knew I was dead. He was like me, but I didn't need his help. I could do this on my own. I started walking a bit faster.

"Dead Guy," he said again, and I felt something grab my shoulders. "Hey, common."

I turned to face him. The guy— Rowley— had one hand on my shoulder, the other at his side. The rest of him was four feet off the ground.

Chapter 3

I knew he was dead, but the sight still shocked me. Being four feet above the ground, he was floating eye level with me. It was weird, yet it made sense. He was more like the stereotypical ghost than I was. But how could he float while I could only walk?

"Well someone just fell off the bridge," Rowley noted, seeing my expression. "I'm guessing you weren't a psychic."

"No," I agreed, still gawking a little. "How are you doing that?"

"Walking's for losers," he smiled to me. "Come on."

I didn't move. "Who's Clyde?"

Rowley shrugged. "A medium."

I was about to ask when I remembered. A medium: people that can see the dead. I remembered there were tons of them around the world, most of them probably fake. I knew the same way I knew what a car was, what country Chicago was in, and two plus two. I knew everything I knew when I was alive, just not my memories.

"Can he find my body?" I asked.

"Oh yeah," Rowley grinned, "he's the boss. He'll explain it."

21
Dead

In the end, I let Rowley lead me to this Clyde person. We went through a countless number of streets, alleys, and traffic jams. It was about early evening, which meant rush hour in Chicago. Though I was aware of Rowley being dead, I still wasn't used to the way he moved. Half the time he was upside down, sideways or on his back. Being able to float and all, he casually swayed over pedestrians and around cars, while I had more trouble on the ground.

"So," Rowley started, "have you figured it out yet?"

I looked at the ghost floating eye level with me. "What?"

"Have you figured out why we're here?"

I thought about it, "Are you asking me the meaning of life?"

"No," Rowley interrupted, frowning. "I mean, we're dead."

"I know."

"So do you know why we're still here?"

I thought again. "Doesn't this happen to everyone who dies?"

"No, no, no," Rowley insisted, like I had voiced some huge misconception. "This," he gestured at everything, "is not the afterlife. This is nothing like the afterlife. The real place you go after you die is a whole lot cleaner, and nicer, and better than all this. Only some people end up here."

22
Dead

"Well we did," I pointed out.

"Not everyone knows why people end up in purgatory," he started, crossing his legs in the air. "They say it has something to do with choice."

"Choice?" I didn't know how I could have chosen this. I could have, but certainly didn't remember it.

"Well, only some people get to choose. Bad people can't choose purgatory," Rowley explained.

Purgatory. I'd heard that word before. Didn't that have something to do with religion? "So we're in limbo?"

"Yeah. You know, the *not*-resting place. You don't go up, you don't go down, you stay here," he continued as he gestured at the streets, "where we are now. Purgatory."

I looked around us. "It doesn't look like a place for dead people." This was still Chicago, the same place I apparently grew up in. How could it be a 'resting place' when there were, like, two million living people here?

"Say we're both alive, and we're standing here fighting over something dumb like a million bucks," he started, floating away from me, "and I've got a gun." He made a small pistol with his thumb and index finger and took aim.

"But what does this have to do with purgatory?"

"Bang!" Rowley shouted. "You're dead."

"Thanks for the heads up," I mumbled.

"So your body collapses," he pointed at the ground, "and your spirit starts spazzing out, like you were a few minutes ago."

I remembered how I climbed out of my body, barely aware of what had happened. I nodded.

"And if you didn't get purgatory," he continued, coming to my side and putting an arm around my shoulder, the other hand stretched out toward the sky, "you look up at the sky and just kind of— fade." Rowley finished, looking up at the sky with a sense of longing.

"Fade?" I repeated. "Into nothing? Then what happens?"

"You go on," he answered, as if it was obvious. "You know, heaven, the big floating place in the sky, the final resting place, the *real* afterlife." Rowley pointed up with his hands. I realized he was talking about the place every ghost was supposed to go.

"But *we* didn't fade," I pointed out. "*We* ended up here." And according to Rowley, I 'chose' purgatory.

"No one really knows for sure," Rowley replied. "No one remembers it. They say it's something we gotta do, or someone to say goodbye to," he shrugged, "you know, before we move on. That's why purgatory's on earth."

I didn't have a memory. I didn't know what I was supposed to do. "How do you know what the reason is?"

"I don't know," Rowley said, pushing forward. "You just know, you know?"

No, I didn't know.

"What are you here for?"

Rowley actually stopped, hanging above my head as he watched the tops of the buildings reach for the sky.

"That's my problem, Dead Guy."

"Oh," I replied, dropping it. I changed the subject, "What if the people that fade don't go 'up?' How do you know they don't go— you know, down?"

Rowley turned back to me, his face a mixture of amusement and fear. "Trust me Dead Guy, you don't wanna know."

"What happens to them?"

He cracked a smile. "Honestly, I hope you never have to find out."

Chapter 4

Being dead, you'd think I would have lost my survival instinct. Sadly, this was not the case. It took me a while to get used to crossing the road while there was traffic. I kept looking both ways before I crossed the street, as if the cars could still hurt me. I couldn't wait for the regular crosswalks because I was trying to keep up with Rowley. It wasn't much of a problem for him because he was able to go over most cars without a problem. I, on the other hand, was pulverized by various mobiles on several occasions. It didn't hurt of course, but it certainly wasn't pleasant.

"Hey Dead Guy, why are you doing that?" Rowley asked as I pull myself up yet again.

"Doing what?" I replied, no dirt on my clothes to wipe as I got back up for the third time.

"Falling down. Doesn't that get annoying after a while?"

"Like I have a choice," I mumbled, continuing across the street.

"You mean you're one of the special-ghosts that can move stuff?"

"Special-ghosts?"

"You know: possess people, move objects, let others see and hear you," Rowley explained. "You're probably too young to have seen any of those yet, but you will."

Huh, *him* calling *me* young. I wasn't psychic, but I knew I was older than him. Then again, depending on how many years he'd been dead, he was technically older than me. "I can't move anything, and I can't fly either."

"Ok, *this* is not flying," Rowley started, gesturing at himself. "It's levitation."

"Sure." I rolled my eyes.

"Whatever. We're here," Rowley replied, sticking his tongue out.

Safe on the sidewalk, I looked to the huge skyscraper towering over us. It was taller than the other ones I had seen so far. It didn't bring back any memories, but I got the feeling it was something important.

"And so this Clyde guy lives here?" I asked, looking up.

"Well he lives in an apartment," Rowley told me, gazing up, "but this is where he works. Since you're stuck on the ground, we'll have to take the elevator." He weaved through people so fast I almost had to trot to keep up with him. Before I knew it, Rowley was halfway through the glass, and I was squished up against the front wall of the building.

"Hey!" I yelled, trying to grab the guy's shirt or something. Rowley, if anything, was a few years younger than I was. He was also a pretty light kid— no pun intended. But the guy was stronger than me, despite his looks. Or was I just really weak? "What are you doing?"

"Huh?"

Rowley's face poked back through the glass, confused. "Whassup?"

"I already said I can't do— *that*." I gestured at his half-in, half-out body. "What are you trying to do?"

"Wait." He came back outside, sawing his arm in and out of the building. "So you mean you can't do this?"

"No," I replied, "I can't move through stuff."

"Oh. Well, then Clyde's definitely going to wanna see you." He led me to the actual building entrance, where I managed to slip through the doors with living people. Rowley followed, choosing to float through the glass instead. I couldn't tell if he was showing off or if it was some kind of instinct.

"How do you do that?" I finally asked as we headed toward the elevator.

"How do you *not* do that?" he replied, frowning, "Seriously, I don't think that's normal."

"Dead people aren't normal," I smiled to myself.

"You'll get used to it," he grinned. There was more silence.

"Dead Guy?"

I looked up. "Yeah?"

"How'd it happen?"

I glanced at the elevator buttons. "How'd what happen?"

"You know," Rowley prodded, gesturing at myself, "you. How'd you die?"

I was silent for a minute. I wondered how to explain it, or if I even could explain it. "I'm not sure."

"What'dya mean you're not sure?" Rowley exclaimed, looking at my blood-covered jacket and bashed up face. "You don't look like you died in your sleep."

"No," I said, more agitated than I meant it to be, "I was killed, stabbed to death."

Rowley snorted, "You were stabbed? That's a new one. Who did it?"

I paused, unsure how to word this. "I don't know."

Rowley frowned, "Well what was happening before that?"

"I don't know."

"What were you doing?"

"I don't know."

"Well where were you?"

I shrugged. "I don't know."

"Well what *do* you know?" he asked impatiently.

I paused again, looking at him. "I don't know."

Rowley considered this. He tilted his head, unsure, "You don't remember anything?"

Again, it'd be convenient if my memory came back about now. I wanted the missing pieces to fall back into place, I wanted to remember. But again, nothing came. It felt as if nothing would ever come.

"Nothing," I replied, shrugging.

Rowley hung in the air silently. "Oh," he said at last, finally getting it. "Then that— that sucks." We continued up the elevator for what seemed like forever. This Clyde guy must be high up in the company.

"This guy can find my body, right?" I asked, breaking the silence. My body was the only identity I had left, and if we could find that, we could find my family, friends, maybe even see my funeral.

"Oh yeah," Rowley replied, perking up a little. "Trust me, no one knows their way around better than this guy."

Chapter 5

"Hey boss," Rowley smiled, poking his head into someone's private office.

Peering through a glass window, I saw a man sitting at a large wooden desk. He was in his late thirties, a bit young to have his own office in my opinion. I was also surprised he was working this late. I guess he must have an important job. He was absorbed in his work, and all I could see was the top of his slick brown hair. It was short, but just long enough to curl out from his neck. I could also make out the rims of thick, square glasses. I was a surprise they didn't slide off his nose. He was dressed for work, a casual suit.

Behind him was another man standing against the wall. This one was older than the businessman, maybe sixty— seventy-ish? He was a living skeleton, tall and lean with a layer of skin on top. He was dressed in a fine suit, a black one with a clean undershirt that made him appear even paler than he already was. His hair was like his body, long and thin. It was an equally startling black that stretched down to the tip of his chin. He wore large reflective sunglasses, like a security agent. I couldn't see his eyes, so I had no clue where he was looking.

The man at the desk finally looked up from his work. "Rowley, I wasn't expecting you," he said in greeting. The man glanced at the clock, "I thought we agreed to wait until I finished work."

"There's a guy outside who wants a favor," Rowley explained, gesturing toward the door, "a dead guy."

"Of course," the man nodded. "Alder?"

The skeleton man crossed the room, passing through the desk as he did. He got the door for us.

When the door opened to the office, I got my first decent look at the inside. The room was fairly large, completely separated from the hallway with a glass door. On the opposite end, the entire back wall was another window showing the Chicago streets below. Whoever this medium was, he certainly knew how to make a living.

As I entered the room, the man at the desk looked me over. I stopped next to Rowley, allowing the medium to get a look at me. The man's eyes gleamed, his eyebrows went up and he gave a single nod. I had forgotten about the blood on my shirt. The thick-rimmed specs continued to look me up and down. The eyes narrowed, and I was beginning to feel like this was a bad idea. Before I could say anything, the man suddenly smiled and gave a short laugh.

"This is an interesting visitor," he said to Rowley, eyes still on mine. "What on earth happened to you?"

"Yeah, fresh off the street," Rowley added, not fazed by the man's reaction. "This is De—" he stopped, realizing that name probably wasn't the best choice. "This is DG."

"D-G," he repeated, the words foreign on his tongue. Then he smirked to himself. "You must have had interesting parents."

"Um, yeah," I stuttered, giving an unsure smile. I didn't know my parents, so I wasn't sure whether or not to be offended.

He laughed. Whether it was at me or his joke, I couldn't tell.

"Well," the man stood up, shifting to a more casual manor, "I'm Clyde Harrison, insurance agent of Living Well, Inc." He came over and shook my hand. "You're a new spirit, I presume? I'm sorry for your loss."

"I—" my hand was barely out of my pocket before it was being pumped up and down by his own. I looked down at our grasped hands. This living person was able to touch me. His hand was warm, an odd type of heat given off his living palms. I guessed it wasn't him being extra warm, but I was just cold now. Still, we were able to shake hands. Was this supposed to happen?

"It's a natural talent, among others," Clyde explained, noting our handshake.

"Well— nice to meet you, Mr. Harrison," I finally managed. "I'm—" I glanced back down at our hands, unsure. DG, it was the best I had at the time. After all, it's what I was: a Dead Guy. "I'm DG."

"You seem incredibly new to all this," he repeated, chuckling a bit. "If you have any questions, feel free to ask me or Alder." The dude in the back gave me a nod. "And call me Clyde."

"Ok, Clyde," I said back.

"So Rowley, tell me about this boy," Clyde went on. He headed back toward his desk and fell into his chair. He then pulled out a pen and paper. "You don't usually bring guests."

"Well, yeah," Rowley piped in. "But I found him on the street like that. Can't float, can't move stuff, can't do anything."

"Not that we didn't already go over that," I frowned.

"You're new," Clyde said to me, swiveling his desk chair toward. "You're still making an adjustment from old life. Depending on how recently you were separated from your body, talents like your friend Rowley has," he gestured toward Rowley floating at my side, "are things that are going to take time. Nothing to worry about."

Adjustment? I didn't have anything to adjust from. But these two didn't know that. Besides, I didn't intend on being here long enough to be like Rowley. I wanted to find my body, my memories, and go wherever the dead are supposed to go.

"I'm not too concerned about learning all that," I replied, glancing at Rowley. "I'm trying to find my body."

Clyde straightened up. "Oh, still in mourning? I see. That's perfectly doable," he flipped the paper in front of him to a blank side, clicking his pen. "Where did you last leave it? Bottom of a lake? Hospital? Car accident?"

I glanced at Rowley, unsure. "I— it was taken by an ambulance, I think. It's probably in some hospital."

"I see," he replied, writing something down. "Cause of death?"

Murder.

The words formed in my mouth, but I held my tongue. I was murdered. But the sentence wouldn't come out. To say so would bring too many questions, questions to which I didn't know the answers. Why would someone murder a teenager in broad daylight?

"It was an accident," I finally said uneasily. "A really bad accident."

"Hmm," Clyde frowned to himself, jotting more things down. "Can you describe this accident for me?"

I thought about it. "No."

"All righty," he mused, eyebrows going back up. "Any family I should know about?"

I hesitated. "No."

Clyde raised an eyebrow. "I see," he said again. I waited for him to ask more questions, but he only made a few more notes and added the paper to a drawer in his desk. "I'll see what we can come up with."

That was it? I looked at Rowley, but he only gave me an encouraging nod. I guess with all the news coverage we have today, finding a body wasn't that hard.

"I'll let you know by tomorrow," Clyde went on, flashing a smile. "I get out of here in a few minutes. The living need their sleep, you know."

"Yeah," I replied, not sure if that was a joke.

"Thank you for stopping by," he added, going back to his work. "And thanks for bringing DG over, Rowley."

"Sure thing," Rowley nodded, floating toward the door.

I glanced at the door nervously, "I—"

Clyde looked up suddenly. "Oh, of course," he smiled apologetically. He gestured to the ghost in black.

The dead man straightened up and went to the door—passing through the desk again, I might add. He reached for the doorknob and twisted it, opening it as easily as a living person. I couldn't help but stare at him.

"I'll look through my resources and see what comes up," Clyde assured me. I whipped my head back around toward his voice, nodding as I walked through the door. "See you tomorrow," he waved. I nodded again.

I left the room after Rowley, and the bodyguard shut the door.

Chapter 6

Harrison

Clyde Harrison watched his visitors go, the newcomer glancing at him one final time before exiting. The door closed, and Clyde returned to his desk. He smiled to himself, beginning to scoop his things into his bag.

"Kids these days," he said to himself. "This is going to be an interesting case, I can tell you that."

"He's hiding something."

It was Alder who had spoken. The dead man's voice was gruff for one with such a thin build. His hidden eyes locked onto Clyde as he stepped up to the desk, waiting for a response. Clyde took his time packing. Lately, his dead friend had been overreacting to quite a lot of things.

"He's certainly unsure of himself," Clyde answered, smiling to himself as he packed. "Peculiar, but he didn't look like he was trying to pull anything."

"He avoided the topic of family, and his legal name," Alder theorized. "It could be a plot."

"He's confused," Clyde wheeled back to face Adler. "Can you blame him?"

It was true this newly dead soul was going to be a strange customer. Clyde had seen enough fidgety ghosts to learn how to smell a secret. DG was hiding something from them, and Clyde could accept that. On the other hand it was rather suspicious, and Clyde Harrison was not a man without enemies. It was only natural Alder would be suspect of any newcomer. They might have to keep an eye on DG.

"Yes, the afterlife seems to be a very new world for our DG," Clyde perceived, turning away. Yet Clyde wasn't thinking about the new ghost. He rummaged through his bag, retrieving a ratty smartphone with a long crack across the screen. Clyde unplugged it from the portable charger and gave it a shake. He smacked it against the desk then tried the power button. "Hm, still doesn't work," he muttered to himself. "I'll have to take it in."

"He's been lying to our faces," Alder pointed out. "He doesn't trust us, why should we trust him?"

Clyde stood up with his things, ready to go home. He simply shrugged. "The boy is no threat."

"Still," Alder went on. He wasn't convinced of anything. "He's the fourth mysterious death this year."

Deaths were not new in such a big city. Murders barely made a few lines in the news. But every now and then, a story would come along that didn't add up. There had been others before DG, tales of mystery deaths without a proper cause. They had all been framed to look like suicides, drownings or car failures. Clyde had seen it far too many times. Accident, the boy had said. It was rather unlikely. It wouldn't take long for the police to determine that it was murder.

The real question was why. These recent accidents had seemed far past the capabilities of the average killer. They were beyond normal, paranormal.

"From what he's told us, he knows his death was supposed to look like an accident." Clyde nodded, looking at Alder, "but not very convincing, from the looks of it. Would he recognize his killers?"

"No," Alder assured, "but if he can recall his memory, he might be helpful."

"Yes," Clyde replied, more to himself than Alder. But they would have to be careful. If there truly was a supernatural element in this death, then DG could still be in danger.

"Do you want me to question him?" Alder asked, looking at his friend. Clyde shook his head.

"No. For now the boy will need our guidance, and protection." Clyde started for the door, the image of Rowley's new friends swirling in his mind. "I'm not taking any risks with this one."

DG's murderer would be after him. Once killer found the body they'd go and look for the ghost. Clyde was certain they would cross paths again very soon, though he was not thrilled about making enemies. Still, he would protect this new spirit. Hopefully, with DG's help, the murderer could be taken care of.

Chapter 7

DG

"So what'dya think?" Rowley asked as we headed back outside. The sun was just starting to sink into the horizon and the street lamps prepared for the night with their soft glow.

"Clyde?" I asked, frowning, "I— I don't know." I hadn't gotten any answers from that guy. I didn't know any more than I had before I went in there. It felt wrong.

"Ah don't worry," Rowley cut in, seeing my expression. "He's a fast talker. A bit confusing, but he's good."

"He seems know a lot of dead people," I noted. "Kind of a weird hobby."

"Well, he's an insurance agent," Rowley explained. "He knew most of the people when they were alive. When they die and get confused and stuff, like you," he glanced at me, "then he directs them."

"So has there ever been anyone like me before?" I asked looking at him.

"A no-memory ghost?" Rowley asked. "No, you're weird." He flipped upside down. "Why didn't you tell him how you died?"

I looked back down, frowning. "I don't know a whole lot about it myself." I thought about it. "I didn't lie about it."

Technically, I didn't. And if he was as good as Rowley kept promising, then he'd find out by tomorrow whether I explained everything or not.

As we turned the corner, I glanced at our reflection in the store window. I couldn't help but stare. How come we had reflections in the first place if we were dead? I stopped to look at myself.

"Rowley," I asked, "is this normal?"

My bruises were gone. My forehead was free of blood, and my jacket was un-blood-stained. I looked completely normal, besides the whole dead thing. How long had I been walking around like this? And more importantly, how did this happen?

"Huh?" Rowley was still upside down, floating over to see. "Oh yeah, you're adapting."

"Weird," I mumbled to myself.

"Yeah," Rowley smiled. "You reverted from dead you to just— you. It's 'your inner mental image' or something like that."

I looked back at the reflection, the unfamiliar face mimicking my own. "And is that bad?"

"If you had your hopes set on walking around all bloody and gross forever, than it's devastating," he smirked in reply. "Actually, some ghosts never revert back to normal. So I guess it's really a good thing for you. Come on."

42
Dead

As the sky turned black, less and less of the living walked the streets. Some I could barely tell they were dead, while others dressed like hospital patients. I was surprised how many dead were in Chicago. As the hours went by, I realized a body would be tired by now. A body needed sleep, but my soul was as awake as it had always been. I knew ghosts supposedly came out at night, and I was beginning to understand why: it was our time to rule the town.

The dead certainly made me feel less alone. Groups wandered and cackled through the streets, and Rowley and I weaved through them.

After getting the info on the dead, I knew what I had to do. If I found my body, maybe I'd be able to pass on. But that was going to take time. I glanced back at my floating counterpart, nodding and smiling at passing dead while humming some kind of tune. I was getting the hang of the streets. It seemed I could get along pretty well in the afterlife.

By the time we got to the next street, the city was packed with ghosts. The dead were about as diverse in the city as Rowley and Alder. Some floated, while others walked like me. Most passed through walls, but one or two had the ability to open doors.

Each seemed to hold some story, some memory of death clinging onto their clothes. Some wore hospital gowns, but few had the gory blood-stained and near death sickness look you'd see in the movies. Not a lot of ghosts had "adapted" like Rowley and I had. Laughs, screams and howls echoed down the streets while the living went onward, oblivious.

"Are we at the hospital yet?" I asked, sticking close. Rowley insisted Clyde would have my body tracked down by morning, but I wanted to do some of my own work. I highly doubted any living person would be allowed to explore a morgue or anything at will, so I decided Rowley and I would. My body was taken in an ambulance, so it had to be in a hospital. Since Rowley knew the town, he was taking me to any possible places my corpse could be. This hospital would be the first on our tour of all Chicago's medical care facilities.

"Nope," he chirped.

I looked up and down the street, trying to estimate the distance. "Wouldn't it be easier if we took a bus?"

"Maybe for you," Rowley looped in front of me, cutting me off. "You'd stay inside. I'd fly right out the back end." He turned and began to lead again, "Buses are too fast for me."

I couldn't argue with that. Walking would make the journey a lot longer than necessary, but I guess it didn't matter. I had all the time in the world now.

We passed an apartment building, one that seemed haunted. An old women sat on the doorstep, holding two chains bound to the steps of the door. As we passed, she screeched and waved her locks at us like a dog at an intruder.

"These other people are— interesting," I thought out loud.

"You'll get used to it," Rowley told me, smiling and waving at the howling woman.

"Ok," I decided, concerned. "But what's wrong with them?"

"Some people get pretty territorial," he shrugged. "When you lose contact with your friends and family, sometimes the physical place is all you have left."

"You don't say," I replied, glancing back at the hag.

"It's why dead people haunt things. They want their lives and stuff. They'd do anything to get them back," Rowley went on, looking ahead. "That's part of the reason why they're here."

I looked over at him. "Where'd you get that?"

"Clyde. He's figured out a lot of this stuff."

"Oh."

You'd think if heaven was everything people said it was, no one would want to stay in this dump. I guess some people couldn't let go.

"Anyway," Rowley cut in, curving to float in front of me, "we should keep moving."

Chapter 9

The hospital in front of us was an older one, but certainly in working condition. Beyond an old chain gate, a tall white building loomed in front of us. The sign in front read *West Ford Hospital*. I turned to Rowley.

"Do you think it's in there?"

"There are quite a lot of hospitals in the city," he replied. "But this one specializes in adolescent and emergency care."

We headed toward the door. "And how do you know that?"

Rowley had already zoomed up the path, waiting at the entrance. "Dead people learn a lot about hospitals."

Once at the door, an unseen problem suddenly occurred to me. Rowley could get in easily; walls weren't a problem for him. But they were for me. I turned to him.

"Great, now how do I get in?"

Rowley tilted sideways at the door, one hand holding his chin in thought. "I didn't think of that." He floated around the door, trying to pick out some sort of open entrance. "They always have people working. You could wait."

"In the middle of the night? Nobody will be coming in or out for hours," I told him. Rowley kept looking, but clearly a hospital wouldn't leave an opening big enough for a human body. They had to keep out unauthorized visitors.

Rowley frowned, still searching the door. "Do you think you can squeeze under the crack or something?"

I looked at him. "Are you crazy?"

"Fine," Rowley decided. "I'm going in to find a way for you. Stay here and look from the outside."

"Fine," I agreed, and a moment later Rowley had slipped through the walls of the building.

The hospital may have been old, but it was secure. I walked around the outside of the building, searching for any vents or even air ducts that might allow me to get in. By now I'd assume it was anywhere from 1-3 in the morning, the moon brightly shining on the brick walls of the building. I remembered there weren't any stars in the city because of light pollution. But no matter, I didn't need light in my path anymore.

"Hey," I reminded myself, "at least you know you won't get mugged."

I walked on the grass, examining the perimeter. Almost three quarters around I finally spotted a window. Hopeful, I went over to it. Pressing my hands up against the glass I looked to see if there was any way through. Like all other times my hands were incapable of passing through the window. I stepped back, turning toward the city. Maybe I could find some ghost that could move things, maybe get him to open the door for me. I snorted, turning back to the hospital. That was a dumb idea. To think the dead just sat around, waiting to get doors for people.

Frustrated, I kicked the wall. My foot bounced back off, just like it always did. Why was I stuck on the ground? Why was my soul this invisible thing no one could see, yet somehow able to be stopped by a dumb piece of cement? What the hell was wrong with me?

"Are you sure it's safe to be out here?"

I froze. Who else was out here at two in the morning? Was it spirits? I started to follow the sound.

"Of course it is. No one's gonna catch us. They don't expect people to break into a hospital."

This second voice belonged to a guy. The other had been a girl's. But break into a hospital? They must be alive, or why else would they be worried about security? I rounded a corner, still no sign of the people.

"Rico," the other voice said, the female one. "Do you think that—?"

"He's dead," the male voice said, cutting her off. "He's not here anymore."

I paused. Were they looking for someone in the hospital? Someone who had died? Someone whose body was in the hospital? I didn't want to think it, and I didn't want to jump to conclusions but—

I went on walking, a little faster than before. There was more talking, but I couldn't catch what was said.

"The Reaper won't be too happy with us."

Reaper?

The male voice sighed. "He won't find out."

"But we can't leave this the way things are. We should finish it. It's what he'd want us to do!"

I halted, pulling up just before the next corner. These people definitely knew someone who had just died. But that could be anyone, anyone at all. I shouldn't jump to conclusions.

I turned the corner, but the people were gone. To my surprise, the window was actually open. I couldn't help but feel a little shocked. Had these people really broken into a hospital? It wasn't like it was closed to visitors in the daytime. Was this some sort of criminal gang?

I went over and peered inside. The murmur of human voices was audible, but I couldn't make out what they were saying. I saw the bottoms of feet make their way across the room. I pressed my ear as close as I could to listen in for more. But before I could, I heard the clear sound of the door click shut.

I waited. There wasn't any more sign of the living beings, almost like they weren't there. But I had heard people. They had been right there!

"Hello?" I asked slowly, climbing through the window. They probably couldn't hear me. They were alive, weren't they? Besides, I couldn't hear their voices anymore.

I walked into a waiting room, my surroundings illuminated by the glow of the moonlight. I could see where I was, I could maneuver without bumping into anything, but the only light was from the window. Chairs were lined against three sides of the room, the forth side a reception desk. It was closed now, but that didn't necessarily mean it was empty.

"Hello?"

Out of the corner of my eye, something moved. I turned, and for the first time I noticed a door at the other end of the room. I remembered the two voices walking out the other way, out a door they had shut a while ago. But this one was wide open, as if someone had left it by mistake. The incoming moonlight was on my side of the room, making the open door greatly resembled a black hole. It looked like an open mouth ready to swallow me up. It looked like it was left open on purpose.

Someone was waiting for me.

I pushed that thought out of my head. "Rowley?"

Cautiously, I headed towards the door. Rowley had already gone inside. So he could've opened the door somehow, right? Maybe?

"Rowley this isn't funny," I called, more angry than fearful. Rowley didn't call back. Nobody did. There was no breath to quicken, no heart to beat faster, but I could feel my soul, my *being*, grow tight and nervous.

I poked my head into the next room. I double checked the area, but no one was there. Instead, I found a staircase. It was the emergency stairs for when the elevator was broken. I must have been on the ground floor, because the stairs didn't go down. They only climbed up, up and up until they disappeared into the darkness.

Somebody wanted to meet me.

I tugged on my sweatshirt, trying to snap out of it. The worst had already happened to me, there was nothing more that could be done. The hospital was closed, and the only people that could see me were equally harmless. There was nothing bad that could happen to me. I headed up the stairs.

Like everything else in the building, the stairs were old. But they were silent. There was no eerie echo to resound with each step, no pitter patter of feet to be heard. I had no weight to pitter patter with. If anything the silence was worse, making the endless pause feel drawn out with each step into the unknown. I was alone, in nothing, climbing up towards nothing. There was no light to guide me, no way to tell if I was even there. Then the whispers started to come.

Softly, very softly, faint moans could be heard echoing from another room. The rasp of a gruff voice droned from the nothingness, ranting about some unknown topic. The chorus of weeping chimed with the never-ending gossip, keeping the manifold of voices from being picked up.

There were spirits in this building, spirits I had never considered meeting. They were everywhere, on each floor, with each step, resounding with their lamenting cries of death. I couldn't see them, but their cries broke through the walls of the stairway, sounding from the numerous rooms I passed. Their voices moaned together as one, no way to tell which ghost said what.

Grandma, I don't like the hospital.

I straightened up, turning around. That voice was different from the others. It was right there, as if it had spoken to me, in me. It sounded young, but familiar. It was the voice of a child. It was almost as if I recognized that voice. It sounded like someone I knew.

But who? I didn't know anybody. I shook my head again, quickening my pace. This was a hospital. People died in a hospital. Of course there would be spirits from years of loss. That voice was merely louder than the others.

Then again, why did it sound like me?

Chapter 10

A block of light soon came into sight. It wasn't bright, but it was lighter than a pitch black staircase, that's for sure. Another door had been left open, waiting for me to arrive. As I climbed the last few steps, the voices echoed less and less. Their whispers fell to a hush as I entered the next room.

It was another hallway, a prep room for surgery, I think. This one had emergency lights, but their dim glow wasn't very helpful. The room stretched out in a curve in front of me, curtained off sections on either side for incoming patients. But no one was there now, and the blocked rooms remained still and silent as the grave. No pun intended.

Whoever had left the doors open wanted me in this room. It sounded crazy, but how else could I have gotten this far? Knowing I couldn't turn back at this point, I continued forward. Despite myself, I still slightly hoped to run into Rowley.

Ghost or no ghost, it didn't matter. I wasn't here to make friends. I was here to find my body. However I found it wasn't important. From here on out I might be able to make my way around the building, find what I needed to find. I wasn't afraid of ghosts because I was one. Any spirit who tried to hurt me couldn't, because we were both dead. Right?

54
Dead

It took a few steps into the room when I suddenly heard the clear sound of sniffling. Something that I thought had vanished at the staircase.

They're just spirits, I told myself, trying not to slow down. It almost sounded funny, *just* dead people. *They can't hurt me.*

As I rounded the corner, the whimpering cries grew louder and louder. The ghost was in this room, I knew that.

It can't hurt me.

One of the curtains was open on the left side, the shadows of a hospital bed barely visible in the light.

Can it?

"YOU!"

The voice boomed, cutting through still air like an arrow. I turned. I knew without thinking the voice had come from the hospital bed. I tried to remain calm. These ghosts were dead, just like me. They couldn't be any worse than myself.

"Yes?" I answered, stopping. Something behind the curtain shifted. It was coming closer. I waited.

"Who are you?" a voice demanded. There was more high-pitched sniffling and the sound of someone angrily trying to cover up tears. The voice was childlike, yet rough like sandpaper. "What do you want? Why you come here?"

It hopped closer. From the light I could make out grey, dirty feet shuffling in the light. They were a dead child's feet: overgrown and mangled.

"I um," I had thought this thing was the one that had lead me here, but I guess I was wrong. "I'm not here to hurt you," I explained, edging closer. "You're the one that left your door open."

"Darla doesn't open doors," the ghost hissed, feet stomping in agitation. "Darla didn't bring you here!"

As if on cue, the door slammed shut and open again. Apparently Darla *does* open doors. Maybe she wasn't aware of that. Either way, she had control of this place. Like Rowley had said, it was this was her territory. I tried to sound calm.

"I'm just passing through."

"Passing through, passing through, he says," the voice continued, chuckling at humor that wasn't there. The feet began to migrate behind the curtain, pacing in frustration. "Lies! Lies, that's what he is. That's what he says last time, says he: 'I'm just passing through.'" It made a horrible imitation of another's voice, unnaturally high and small. "Theys tries to trick Darla, theys think theys so *smart*."

The poltergeist snuffed out the word, angrily switching directions. I watched the feet in wonder, trying to think this through.

"I'm not trying to trick you," I assured, "I swear. I just want to get to the other side."

"Other side, other side," echoed the ghost, laughing. "Other side, theys says. That's all they want, other side. Then theys wants Darla's help: 'help me Darla.'"

The squeaky imitation made me flinch. It was such an off-key sound. This ghost was unsettling, worse than the lady with the chains on the street. But I couldn't go backward. I could only go forward.

I took a step. "I won't need your help. Really, you can just stay there. It's fine."

There was a thrashing behind the curtains. "Fine, fine, fine, fine, *fine!*" the ghost declared, voice stretching and growing and twisting. In a flash, the curtains threw themselves open and Darla was standing there, fury with a face and bloodshot eyes,

"It's all *fine*. It's all *dandy*. Then theys wants your help, your *favor!*"

Her spirit was as equally unnerving as her voice. The ghost bore a torn, mangled lime-green hospital gown stained brown with blood. She was crouching on all fours, like a dog. Hands as gnarled and dirty as the gown, with frizzled yellow hair saturated with dirt and blood that gave her the impression of a deranged poodle. Darla had the face and mannerisms of a child, maybe seven. But her eyes were very, very old.

"Hey," I started, trying to keep her calm, "I didn't—"

"They says they helps Darla, they promises," the ghost went on, hangnail feet crawling back and forth. Her hands stayed tucked securely in her hunched abdomen as she walked. "They says they was good. 'Promises Darla.'"

The imitation was anything but spot on. I crept onward, wondering if I could sneak by without her noticing. But the door on the other end was closed. I turned around to exit the way I came, when that door slammed shut behind me. I don't know how, but I knew Darla had done it. I was trapped.

"They promises. But they *left*. They left Darla!"

First she wanted me out of here, now she wanted to have a chat. Was this ghost telling the truth, or was it just delusional? Had this mysterious person left because they were alive and couldn't see her? There wasn't any way I could tell.

"I— Darla, I'm sorry," I apologized, trying to ensure the spirit understood me. "I don't know—"

"Theys say theys wants to help, but it's the *blood* they're after!"

She tore her gaze from the opposite wall and bored her eyes into me, as if looking could convey the intensity of the statement. She waited a moment, to see if I understood the message. But I could only look back bewildered. I had no idea what she was talking about.

"Theys tooks it," she howled, yellow eyes glaring. The emergency lights flickered and glowed, almost bursting with light. "Theys tooks my blood! And now *you* wants it. Get out! *Get out!*"

At her words, Darla lunged at me. Shocked, I scrambled backward, running and tripping at the same time to get away. Darla charged forward, barreling straight through any object that stood in her way. The whole time she was screaming like the banshee she was.

I ran, backing away to get as much distance between me and that thing as possible. I scrambled over carts and desk chairs, but space was running out. And Darla wasn't slowing down.

I took a step back, but my foot reached the back wall instead. Taking my first instinct, I rolled to the side, dodging impact as Darla pounced through the wall and into the next room. Getting to my feet I kept running, going back down the other way to the open door.

It wasn't far, thirty feet, maybe less. I was almost there now; I could get back out.

"Yous can'ts have it! Yous can'ts trick Darla. Yous can never takes it from Darla. Never!"

The door. I was almost there, almost out. Before I could blink, the little monster slid in front of the exit, blocking my freedom.

I skidded to a halt right before she could touch me. For a kid, that girl was fast. How?

I heard a scream, and moved before Darla could pounce again. I looked to either side, trying to find another way out.

A window. There was a window open to my right, partially hidden behind one of the hospital beds. I didn't know how far up I was, but it was a chance I had to take. I *was* already dead.

The window was tight, but I just might manage. I squeezed myself through it, headfirst, hoping I was able to make it. I had to be able to make it.

"You can't escape Darla! Darla will find you."

With a twist, push, and a few seconds of kicking, I had gotten through the window. I was free, and I fell.

Chapter 11

When you crash to the ground at unsafe speeds, being numb can have its perks. But can I say I never wanted to fall from a fifth story hospital window ever again? Yes, I can.

I was aware of wind. I knew it was rushing past me, around me, but it didn't affect me. It didn't tousle my hair, move my clothes. It was just wind.

I hit the ground head first, rolling a few times before I found myself sitting upright. Yet another perks of being dead. I got to my feet and ran from the hospital until I was in the parking lot. I wasn't out of breath, nor was I in pain, but whatever kept me going seemed to be tired.

I fell to the ground, resting myself while I watched the hospital. I could only imagine Darla would tumble out the window after me. Would that ghost really chase me through the entire city, the entire world? I hadn't even done anything. She was crazy.

And what did she mean by 'blood?' She didn't have blood, she was dead. It must have been made up. Or maybe someone had done something to her when she was alive. Somebody may have killed her.

Like somebody killed me.

"Hey DG!"

"WHAT," I yelled suddenly, jumping to my feet and turning around. Before my mind had processed what had happened, Rowley was behind me. He was tucked into a U-shape and clutching his stomach and laughing. "What was that for?"

"I'm just kidding," Rowley chucked, recovering from his laughter. "But you should have seen you face."

"How'd you get over here?" I asked, shrugging off my shock.

"Well I *was* trying to find a way in the hospital," Rowley replied, "but I didn't find anything. So I went looking for you."

"And you didn't find out anything about my death?"

"Well, I can't use a computer and I didn't see a dead you lying around," Rowley explained, shrugging. "Clyde's probably found a file though."

"But if it's in there I want to see it for myself," I sighed, looking away. Maybe there was something left there, like a clue.

"Hey," Rowley said, trying to pick up the mood. "We can go back in and look. It's fine."

"No," I said a little too quickly. "I'm not going back in there."

I quickly explained how I got in and what had happened, following Rowley as we started to drift back towards the inner city.

"She was crazy," I finished, replaying the scene in my head. "She kept going on about how I trying to steal her blood."

"Blood?" Rowley frowned.

"Yeah, she's probably some old mental patient or something," I decided, crossing the street with Rowley leading the way. "I'm surprised she didn't follow me."

"Ghosts are weird like that," Rowley said to me, weaving around a street light. "After a while they get so old they never leave their resting place."

It sounded like ghosts in the movies, like the ones where people move into haunted houses on top of old cemeteries. "You'd think they'd want to get out more."

"Come on, it's their resting place," he explained, "their home, their grave. Anything that has a strong connection to their life helps with their energy. You know how we still get tired when we run even though we don't have a body?"

"Yeah," I nodded.

"It's the same kind of energy that keeps us in purgatory. And the energy gets stronger the closer we are to doing whatever 'thing' we're here for. It's kind of like our motivation. Eventually, a ghost will be so weak they can't leave their life connections without fading away. It's why some are territorial. We get strength from it."

"Oh." I hadn't felt anything like that since I died. So far there had been no sudden urge of 'strength' or something like that. Obviously I still had a lot of looking to do.

As we wandered back down the street, we passed the house with the old woman again. She waved her chains at us, barking and howling. She hadn't moved from her doorstep. How long had she been there? Not just tonight, but the night before, a week ago, a year. Purgatory seemed so long for her.

"What exactly is it about being dead that drives people so mad?" I asked, my eyes still on the woman.

"I guess it depends," Rowley shrugged. "Depends on who you are, what your life was like, how far you'll go."

I listened to him talk, tuning out the shrieks of the city. To think all these ghosts are doing the same thing they did last night, and the night before that. That alone would make me lose it.

"It sucks, staying with your life connections but not truly *being* there. You're unable to interact with it. You miss your life—your home, your family. You get to find out what they'd do without you, and you hate it. And here you've waited for them, walked with them, and yet they don't say *anything*. They can't say anything." Rowley's hands had curled into fists. "And it doesn't matter what you do because they can't hear you. You don't exist. And here you've spent all of death thinking about them, and they never think about you!" Rowley looked like he was shaking, like he might explode. Instead, his body sagged, and his arms dropped. "But you miss them. You'd do anything for them."

I turned away from Rowley, trying to give him some space. I was pretty desperate to find my life, some trace of my memory. Would I go crazy too? Would I be the one waving chains at the neighbors for touching my tombstone? I hadn't given much thought about my future, but I didn't want to be around long enough to find out.

"Let's just find my body," I decided, turning back to the street.

Despite the fact I was one of them, the dead creeped me out.

Chapter 12

It was midmorning when I waited outside the office door. I didn't say much on the way to Clyde's office, or the rest of the night really. Rowley took me to a few more hospitals and a couple of morgues. We didn't find my body, or anything that would give us any more clues. In the end Rowley was right: we had to wait for Clyde. I waited a whole night for the thing I didn't have fingers to do. I guess you could say I was nervous. Who wouldn't be? It wasn't that I disliked Rowley's friend. I was probably just nervous to learn about my life. Who wouldn't be?

The hallway had been empty this morning, just like the last time I came here. I didn't give much thought to Clyde's job, but I suppose he was high up in rank. Why else would someone get their own office?

Rowley was already inside talking to Clyde. The muffled voices of the office seemed to go on longer than normal. It seemed like an hour had gone by when Clyde finally opened the door.

"DG, good to see you again," Clyde smiled as I walked in. "You haven't aged a day."

It was a tad early for bad jokes. We walked in the room together, and I couldn't help but notice someone was missing. "Where'd Alder go?"

"As strange as it sounds, Alder has his own matters to attend to," Clyde explained. "It's not like we're chained together you know."

"Right," I answered, moving to sit down in one of the chairs. Rowley lowered himself, sinking down to hover next to me. "Have you found anything yet?"

"Of course, straight to business," he smiled, settling down and going for some of his notes. I smiled back, but it didn't put me at ease. "I didn't have much to go on, but I looked into recent deaths. Alder has done some work as well."

It'd be nice to hear the ghost's side too, but he wasn't here. I waited.

"And?" I asked nervously. There was too much small talk. Something was missing here.

"Well, DG," Clyde started to apologize. My expression dropped. The agent's business smile fell to sympathize. "I'm sorry, but I believe your story cannot be found."

"It's not there?" I asked in disbelief. "They can't do that. It's against the law."

"I'm sorry," Clyde said again, "but whoever is legally responsible for you doesn't want your information public. Your guardian has withheld personal information. The news has to abide by those kinds of requests, especially from a mourning family."

'Legally responsible,' as if someone still looked after me. It was ironic, considering how much I was on my own now.

"Well the news must have said *something,*" I pointed out, still angry. "They can't just let a— an accident like that slip by."

I almost said murder. It wasn't a huge deal whether Clyde knew or not, but I couldn't admit that I had lied to him. Yet whoever killed me was still out there. Even without giving my picture, someone would have to bring that person to justice.

"I know, someone will take care of the legal work," Clyde assured me. "But I'm afraid they want to keep it from the public eye. I can definitely give it some more research, but it will take time. I have a career to keep up with."

"I know," I sighed, looking away. Rowley gave me a sympathetic shrug that didn't make me feel any better. "But you can't find it? There's no word on a teen death in the area?"

True, he was looking for the wrong thing, but there had to be word somewhere.

"Your case certainly is a strange one," Clyde thought out loud, folding his fingers into a tent as he leaned back, thinking. "I could understand not wanting the press involved— if it were my own child of course. But consider what your family is going through." He looked over at me.

"I don't support your guardian's decision. Unfortunately, there's nothing I can do about it."

"Did you check the obituaries?" Rowley asked, leaning forward.

"That's the thing," Clyde continued frowning. "There are too many deaths reported to pinpoint which one is DG."

"You mean I'm not the only teenager that died this week?" I didn't believe it. I knew people died, but teen deaths—murders— were not that common, even in the city. Surely something must have stood out.

"No, I'm sad to say," Clyde answered, matter-of-factly. "There have been multiple deaths of young people this week. And not many photos."

"Multiple?" I repeated. I had been around town all night and seen half the city. All night, I hadn't seen any other new spirits or any signs another murder had occurred. What was happening?

"Five," Clyde corrected solemnly. "All pictures are being withheld. The police are looking deeply into these investigations. They believe some kind of killer is on the loose."

I looked at him, stunned. Clyde wasn't lying, I knew he wasn't. Yet the words didn't make sense.

"Of course," he continued, pushing his chair back, "two deaths have been proven to be accidents." He stood up and walking around the desk toward me. "If you ask me, it looks like more than mere gang violence."

"Do you think it's a different kind of gang?" Rowley asked, leaning forward. "You know, like before."

Before?

"Those groups have been permanently dispersed." Clyde shot Rowley a serious look.

"What groups?" I asked Rowley, confused.

"Allow me," Clyde said, brushing his comrade off. "DG, if you haven't noticed, the dead have close ties with their old lives. They like to— mingle with their living connections, so to speak. Of course not all psychics have a steady income." He looked down humbly. "Some— most, I might say, have rather unpleasant connections."

He's using them! That's how he does it!

Clyde continued. "And if a spirit were to ask a living person to, say, do away with old enemies—"

I blinked. No one in the room seemed to react to the sudden voice. I had heard it, clear as daylight. I knew there was a voice. I realized— or confirmed, really— that it was my own. I had said that, in my head. But was it real? Was it something from my past, or was I hallucinating? Being dead, I hardly knew the difference.

Clyde had said something else about these gangs. Rowley listened, and I guess it looked like I was too. I tried not to let my true expression show.

"They're hired for revenge," Rowley explained darkly, making a gun with his fingers.

"Exactly, I'm sorry to say," Clyde frowned. "The dead can send some awfully bad requests from the afterlife."

"And you think one of these 'bad ghosts' has something to do with *my* death?" I asked.

"We can look into it," Clyde nodded. "Do you have any reason to think someone would want you dead?"

"I—" I frowned, still in thought under Clyde's gaze. I couldn't tell whether he suspected something or not, but I couldn't give him an answer. None of these thoughts were jogging my memory. And whatever that voice was, it was hardly any evidence.

"I don't think so."

Clyde sighed. "The dead are very good at covering their tracks in these sorts of things." He headed back to his desk, sitting down again. "But I will still look into it, nevertheless."

"Thank you," I said, standing up. "When do you think you'll know?"

Clyde smiled. "These things can take quite a while you know." He rose from his desk and began to make his way to the door. "But I assure you, you will be the first to know if I find anything. Your case is a little trickier than normal DG, but keep on looking."

Rowley had already drifted through the door, and Clyde opened it for me.

"Thanks," I said again, turning to leave.

"Oh, and DG?"

I turned, Clyde looking at me through his glasses.

"If you find anything that could help, anything at all, let me know."

It didn't hurt to lie. There wasn't a knot to form in my stomach. But something inside me still shivered at his words.

"I will."

Chapter 13

"Sorry about your body, dude," Rowley frowned sympathetically as we walked out of the building. I sighed, hands in my pockets. So far the only thing that had given me any clues were the voices nobody else could hear. And even those weren't very helpful.

"It's fine," I shrugged. The two of us were making our way down the street. People walked by us, sometimes even over us, but I had gotten used to it by now. That was the one good thing about being dead: you were invisible. "Does he always take this long to find stuff?"

"No, this is really the first time it's taken him a few days," Rowley shrugged, rolling in the air. "I guess it's just harder because you don't remember anything."

"Yeah," I agreed, looking down the street.

Rowley floated down in front of me as we continued moving forward. "Do you seriously not remember?"

By now I was unfazed by the floating boy in front of my face. "Yep," I agreed. "Nothing."

"Are you sure?" he repeated, frowning.

"I'm sure," I said again, exasperated. I waved him off and continued forward. "I don't know how or why, but I don't."

Rowley remained where he was, staring at me. "Oh."

It was mid-morning. People were bustling about the streets while traffic died down and picked up again. Rowley led the way because he knew the streets better. Every so often people would pick a spot out of everyone's way and set up a little station. Some played, others sang, and some just asked for money. Rowley had told me it was Friday, which explained why it was more crowded than usual. The music was pretty good.

We were halfway down the street when I stopped in front of one the musicians. The guy was having the time of his life, throwing his head back and wailing away on the saxophone. His station was in front of a small coffee shop, one that wasn't too busy. It was a good tune, one you'd blast out of the car radio on a Saturday night. One you'd memorize and listen to over and over.

I knew the song, despite my lack of memories. I knew it by heart. My feet started to walk in time with the beat. I hummed along.

"Rowley, what song is this?" I asked. I knew this song, I knew I did. My companion looked at me.

"This?" he frowned. He stopped to think about it. "Dunno. Why?"

"I think I do." My pace quickened, faster than the beat. I left Rowley where he was standing to sprint toward the musician. I pulled up right in front, eagerly drinking in every note. No one saw me and the player didn't stop to notice, but I was used to that. I could recall the music. I knew each note before it was played, though the lyrics themselves were sketchy. But that didn't matter. This was a part of my life I knew. Right here, right now, was something in front of me that I remembered.

"Good song right?"

"Yeah," I sighed, clapping with the crowd when the song was over. "It sounds older. Do you think Clyde could look it up?" Then I stopped. It wasn't Rowley who had spoken.

A girl was standing right next to me, looking right at me. Her brown eyes stared directly into mine, a gesture I had almost forgotten. She had darker skin, the color of coffee. But I found it wasn't her face I was staring at. It was her clothes.

It looked like someone barfed up a clown onto her clothes. Her orange shirt went well past her belt and ended somewhere around her mid thighs. Around her long dark hair scattered with miniature braids was a thick headband that almost covered the top of her head. It was a splatter of reds, oranges and light off-yellows, like some sort of tie dye. And as if that wasn't enough, she was covered with assorted necklaces. There were seven, ranging from a choker to a long pendant. Gold hoop earrings, chunky wood bracelets and multiple metal rings on her fingers completed the look.

Maybe she was talking to one of her friends, not to me. I must have just overheard her, that's all. I checked again, but the girl was still staring at me. And I mean right at me.

"*Smells like Teen Spirit*. You like Nirvana?" she asked me.

The words ran through my brain, trying to find meaning. That must be the song and the singer.

"Yeah," I replied. If I knew the song, it had to be true. "Yeah, I guess so." Though her clothes were a bit of a distraction, at least she had ok taste in music. Still, most of the time people with that much jewelry were a little—off.

"Ok, so abandoning me for the guy with a saxophone is not cool," Rowley cut in, zooming up next to me. "It hurts my feelings."

"Oh hello," the girl smiled at him. "I'm sorry, your friend just got a little distracted here."

Rowley did a double take. "Wait, are you alive?"

"Last time I checked," she shrugged.

"Ok," I decided, "we need to talk."

Chapter 14

The coffee shop was small, one you'd stumble upon once and never find again. The girl had insisted we go there to talk. I wasn't ready to walk around for five minutes before engaging in conversation, but the shop turned out to be right behind us. All we had to do was walk across the street.

Although you could say it was almost lunch time— brunch time maybe— the place wasn't that crowded. Clusters of tables with chairs here and there were scattered around some low-rise couches and skinny, twisting lamps. It was bright outside, but inside the coffee shop made it feel like evening. The blinds were almost glowing as they filtered out the daylight.

"What is this place?" I asked, looking around.

"It's where I go for lunch. I'll be right back," the girl replied, heading off to the counter to get something.

She was alive. We discovered that on the way here when someone bumped into her. I thought that she might have been dead and didn't know it, like I had. But she was a living person, one who went to coffee shops for something to eat. Personally I hadn't thought about food much since I died. Surprisingly I didn't miss it. I wasn't hungry. Still, it was kind of a relief to interact with a living person.

Even though it wasn't crowded, the few people in the shop were enough to scare normal people away. Groups of young adults took their lunch break in silence, sipping coffee while ensuring their nose rings didn't get in their drink. Older women, too old to be wearing the clothes they had on, shared some kind of pastry and long dreadlocks. In the corner a man sat all by himself, mumbling things to no one in particular. All sound was mostly drowned out by the self-playing piano near the front. I watched as its keys moved automatically up and down to produce some unknown melody.

This place was weird, even for me. I wanted this girl's help, but not if she was a lunatic.

"This is—"

In my mind's eye an image of this cafe appeared. The doors to the coffee shop push open in front of me as I walk in. The memory of a smile was on my lips, laughing even. I could feel in my palm the hand of another as I dragged someone in behind me.

"This is my kind of place."

I stopped in mid-sentence, my mind interrupting my own words. The memory was stronger than the voices at the hospital and in Clyde's office. I had liked it here? The old me had. That meant I'd been here before, maybe multiple times. And who was with me? Would they ever come back here? If anything else I'd have to stay to find out.

"DG? It's what?" Rowley pestered, leaning up to my face. "Not 'perddy' enough for you?"

"It's fine," I brushed him off and walked toward the girl. "Where do you wanna sit?"

"I have a favorite spot," the girl called, coming toward us with a drink and a pastry. She waved us over. Rowley weaved in and out of various groups of people to follow. I came too, but I couldn't help notice how much this girl talked to us in public. I mean, if no one else could see us, talking to us in public seemed kind of crazy.

The coffee shop was built like a house, various rooms leading to others. Each room was painted a different color and had a different theme. People were scattered among the various places, each with a cup or a few plates of food. I followed Rowley as he dashed ahead, almost unable to keep up with him.

"Hey DG, over here!"

I followed through room after room, running until I hit the very last section. It was a light orange color with tie-dyed paintings and turquoise furniture scattered throughout. As I slowed to a walk the music changed, turning from a jazzy beat to something sounding more contemporary. Rowley was standing by the entrance, impatiently waiting for me to get there.

"Here!"

The girl was sitting on a couch, facing the only window in the room. Rowley was floating above her head waving me over. I sat a good distance from our living friend, with Rowley hovering between us.

"Is that spirit there your friend, or are you dead too?" she asked, shifting to face us more. She placed her drink and glass plate on the table.

I couldn't help but be a little disappointed. I had almost hoped that this girl would know me. "Yeah."

"He's a dead guy all right," Rowley answered for me. He rested an elbow on my shoulder. "I'm Rowley, this is DG." He pointed at each of us. "You're a psychic right?"

"It's a gift," she shrugged modestly. "I'm Cleopatra."

It wasn't that big of a surprise; no one else seemed to be able to communicate with us except these psychic mediums. Even if she didn't know me while I was alive, she still might be able to help us.

"Why don't you sit down," she offered Rowley, scootching over on the couch. "There's room here."

"Nah, I don't sit," Rowley said, still leaning on me. "Ever."

I tried to bring the conversation back to the topic. "So, err, Cleopatra."

"Oh everyone calls me Cleo," she smiled as she reached for her cup.

"Cleo," I corrected, "how long have you had this gift?"

"Since forever," she replied. "I've always been happy to help spirits with anything. Except if you need me to give a message, because I'm not the best at that."

"Um, ma'am?" A worker was standing behind the couch, an arm on the backrest. He leaned forward— through Rowley's back, I might add— giving Cleo a peculiar look. "Is there anything I can help you with?"

"Hey, watch where you're going!" Rowley scowled, scrambling out of the way.

"Oh." Cleo looked up as if she hadn't noticed him approaching. "Yes, you appeared to be out of napkins. Could I have one?"

"Right." The worker started to leave, keeping a wary eye on her.

"I'm sorry," she apologized, noticing the look. "I'm having a conversation with some new acquaintances."

"I see," the waiter nodded uneasily, moving faster to get away.

"Don't be alarmed," she urged while still very tranquil. "You can't see them."

The worker left the room, glancing back at the girl who was talking to herself. I looked over at Rowley, who was making an attempt not to laugh.

"She's a keeper," he whispered before Cleo could notice. I'd talk to him later.

"I don't think I have a message for somebody." I glanced back at the waiter. I didn't want her to talk to anyone.

"That's not what we're looking for here," Rowley cut in, coming back to his old spot. "This guy here," he pointed at me, "has lost his memories of his life. Do you know anything that could help?"

"I'm sorry, this is a mistake," I said to Cleo, turning to Rowley. "You probably don't wanna get involved. I'd completely understand."

"Oh it's no problem," Cleo cut in, "honest. I can help you."

"You can!" Rowley smiled.

"You can?" I repeated.

"Of course," Cleo nodded. "It's my occupation." She took out a card and showed it to us, knowing we couldn't touch it ourselves.

"Cleo's Collaborations and Psychic Readings," Rowley read, leaning forward. "I'm guessing this is a side career."

"It's a way to make money for college," Cleo smiled, not recognizing the implied insult. "My sight isn't the only gift I possess."

"Right," I managed without being offensive. I shot a quick glance at Rowley. Yes this girl could see us, but did Rowley really believe in all this? Death was one thing, but 'mystical psychic abilities' was another.

"Come home with me," she went on, standing up. "I can give you a proper reading there."

"Cool," Rowley smiled, lifting up. I followed suit. We had tried intelligence and research, and that hadn't gotten us anywhere— but trying magical powers and crystal balls? Sure, why not.

Chapter 15

"Mother," Cleo called out, entering the kitchen, "I'm taking some spirits up to my room for a reading. Try not to use the microwave."

"Sure dear," a woman called from the counter. She was dark-skinned like Cleo, painting glass figures at the table. "Hello," she greeted the empty space next to Cleo. "I'm sorry, I can only hear you. My daughter's the more gifted one."

"Hi," I replied, following Cleo.

"Nice place you got here," Rowley added, looking around.

"Why thank you." The woman went back to her work. "We just remodeled."

We followed Cleo up some winding stairs. The whole set-up of her home was pretty nice for an apartment. The rooms were decent size with a good balance of furniture. True, most of the apartment was stocked with strange statues and symbols, but at least it all coordinated.

"So your whole family is psychic?" I asked, looking back at the kitchen.

"Only some of us," Cleo told us, reaching the top and heading down a hall. "My father isn't gifted, but he's a believer."

"So how come you aren't rich?" I asked, looking around. It was a nice space, but considering the talent this girl had, it could've been bigger. "How come everyone doesn't believe in you?"

"We don't believe in exploiting of our gifts," she explained, leading us into a room.

"Said the girl in the psychic business," Rowley smirked.

"We will help those who ask, but most people don't listen," Cleo frowned. "Besides, too much fame taints the heart."

The room was a bright peach color, the door replaced with a curtain of beads. Two sides of the room were covered in book shelves. Piles upon piles of thickly bound books were spilling over the shelves. Some were even piled on the carpet, while others were scattered on the messy bed. Besides the literature, various origami and mystical symbols hung from the ceiling, each held in place by strings of yarn. Other objects in the room varied from fancy pots to scrap metal. Cleo also had a guitar sitting in the corner, leaning against a stone gargoyle.

"Please come in," she gestured. In the corner of the room was a low table set with cushions in place of chairs. A tall candle sat in the middle of a bronze tray that was filled with a mixture of ash and sand. She led us to the table, motioning for us to sit down. Rowley remained in the air, hovering crossed-legged a half a foot above his cushion.

"Now," she headed to her massive bookshelf, "what do you recall? Do you know your zodiac sign, blood type, family curses?"

Even if I were alive I wouldn't know this information. And despite my loss of memory I don't think I would have cared.

"No," I answered.

"Anything at all?" she pressed, pulling out a large book.

"No," I said again. "Sorry, but I'm not sure if any of this is going to help."

"Oh don't worry," she told me. Cleo lit the tall candle then flicked off the lights, drawing the window shade. The darkness swept over the room in a hushed silence. Her face seemed to change, growing solemn. The tranquil light faded from her eyes only to be replaced with something hard, something serious. She took her book to the table, sat down and opened it to a random page.

"Before we begin, I want you to try to relax," she instructed. "It will help with the reading." She paused, her dark eyes fixated on my forehead. I suddenly felt self-conscious.

"Is something wrong?"

Cleo didn't respond. She reached out, her dark fingers brushing against the left side of my head between the forehead and ear. "You were bleeding," she told me. It wasn't a question. It was a fact.

"Yes," I replied. "When I first died I had a bruise on my forehead. I was bleeding too."

Cleo seemed confused. "You were stabbed in the front. Yet you fell sideways."

I nodded. "I woke up on my side."

She nodded as well, as if the picture in her mind was coming together. "You were hurt. The killer made you fall. You hit your head." She pressed her fingers against my head. "There's some damage between your temporal lobe and prefrontal cortex." She retracted her hand and rubbed her fingers against her palm, imprinting the memory on her skin. "Retrograde amnesia."

Rowley gasped, "Not his prefrontal cortex!"

Instinctively my hand came up to where she touched me. "What does that mean?"

Cleo closed her eyes and rubbed her fingers against her thumb. "Somehow you hit the side of your head. You had memory damage the day of the incident. Within the last few seconds of your life, you had retrograde amnesia."

I wasn't sure about the first part, but I knew what amnesia meant. "I think I still do."

"Precisely," She nodded. "Because you couldn't remember your life when you died—"

"I can't remember it in death," I finished. "Is there a cure?"

She dropped her hand to her side and looked up at me. "The dead in purgatory are there to heal," she said. "Most likely, your memories will return to you in time."

I remained still. I had expected to feel some relief at the news, yet nothing happened. I didn't want my memories to come back in time. I wanted them now.

"Perhaps we can recover something through the reading," she went on with a hopeful smile.

I nodded. I could try.

She took a deep breath. I watched the breath leave her, feeling as if I was breathing in unison with her.

"Relax," she ordered.

I did. My spirit began to un-tense, and I tried to be at ease.

"How did you die?" she asked, a vacant paranormal sense now present in her tone. The darkness was soothing. And despite being in a stranger's home, I wasn't afraid.

"I was murdered," I replied, the words coming out naturally.

"I see," she nodded, her brown eyes locked onto mine. "Close your eyes."

I obeyed. I felt her warm living hand slide over to clasp mine. I wasn't surprise, or even curious as she lifted our grasp over the tray of ash. With my eyes closed, she lit the tip of a long wooden stick from the candle flame, setting it in it the sand. The flame ignited, smoke wafting up to our grasp. I don't know how I knew this, but I felt it. I wasn't confused. I wasn't afraid. Not my muscles, but my soul, my presence, was relaxed.

"DG," Cleo said, closing her eyes— I felt her do it. The room seemed to grow darker, everything fading but ourselves and the table. Our hands remained clasped, the heat in our grasp growing. "Who are you?"

"Who am I," I repeated. The words felt dragged out of my mouth from an unknown source. The vision of us was fading, a darkness seeping through. It was black, it was vacant. But something was there. I knew something was there.

"Where do you come from?"

I leaned forward, pressing myself into the darkness. I was looking, searching through the void. Something was in there, something was hidden.

"What's your name?"

"What's my name," the voice repeated, something else forcing it to do so. I pushed on, deeper and deeper into my unconscious. Something was there. Something was forming.

"You already have the answers."

I strained to listen. Cleo's voice sounded far off, miles away. I could no longer feel her hand in mine. Somewhere, someone was saying words. But those words no longer held any meaning to me.

There was a sharp chord. An out-of-tune B-flat on the bass guitar that made my ears shrivel up.

"Dude!"

I looked up. A kid was staring at me, his sharp hazel eyes looking confused. I blinked and let out a breath I didn't know I'd been holding.

"Sorry," I managed, *"I guess I was distracted."*

The two of us were in someone's apartment. The light from the muted television flashed in my face. I was sunken into a reclining couch, staring at a kid my age who was sitting crossed-legged on the coffee table. He had wide, bulging eyes that seemed to watch your every move. In his lap was a blue electric bass guitar. Absentmindedly his fingers went back to plucking strings while he continued to stare. If this kid was gonna own a bass, he should learn to play some half-decent chords.

What was I saying? He wasn't just *any* kid, he was my friend. The only friend I'd had since middle school.

What was his name again?

"That bleeding ghost, the Reaper, and all those other things." he summarized. His fingers started to pluck faster and faster as his voice grew more serious. *"You don't usually believe in any of that stuff. Hell, I don't believe in that stuff. But I guess that's the only thing that can explain those deaths."* I got the sense that he was finally starting to believe me. After months of trying to convince him, he was starting to believe me. I don't know how I knew, but he was. He stopped playing for a four-count rest. *"I guess you weren't so bojangled after all, my friend."*

My mind felt muddled. I ignored my friend's insane vocabulary choice. There was something in my gut, something I should have known about, why it was there, but I didn't. Anger. *"I know. That's why I need to act before school starts."*

The guy was perfectly still, apart from his strumming fingers. His wide eyes seemed to look past me, mulling over the options. He struck a final, ending chord and set the bass down.

"What are you gonna do?"

I stood up, looking my friend in the eye.

I'm gonna find him."

Something snapped. The darkness pulled away, the whole void swirling down a dark hole and disappearing. Suddenly the whole scene was clipped from my mind. I tried to look for the kid again, for the apartment. But I couldn't find it. I couldn't find it because there was no apartment and there was no kid. It had all been a vision.

Suddenly, my eyes were open and I was alert. My mouth opened but no breath came out. I was cold, cold for the first time since I had died. My only warmth was the living hand still holding onto mine. The room was back, the world was back. I was staring at Cleo, who looked almost as pale and shaky as I felt.

"Did you," she stuttered, her voice cracking and tired. "Did you find anything?"

Chapter 16

A slow, one-man clap sounded from next to me. It slowly grew into substantial applause. Rowley, who I had completely forgotten about, was clapping for us.

"That. Was. Amazing!" he exclaimed, awe-struck. "How'd you get him to talk in sync with you?"

We listened, too tired to respond. We were in sync? I was too focused on my vision to notice what was happening around us.

"Do it again. No, do me. Only this time make me think I'm a chicken."

"Rowley," I tried to snap. I was too washed out to make it happen. The whole experience was exhausting. I don't know what Rowley saw from his end, but I now knew I'd never doubt Cleo again. "What exactly happened?" I asked, my mind still in a daze.

"You guys were talking in sync and saying stuff about destiny," Rowley started, excited and astounded. "And you were like, staring at each other, and yelling stuff. It was so cool!"

"I think," Cleo started, regaining her strength, "that your murder has something to do with a bigger plot, DG."

We stared at each other, knowing it was true but not understanding how it was possible. That guy in my vision had seemed so familiar. The vision itself was weird. It was like I couldn't act of my own free will, only recreate what I remembered. If I could have, I would have asked him what he was talking about.

"Didn't we say something about blood?" I asked, turning to Rowley. "'I remember hearing something about a ghost bleeding."

"I'm not sure," Cleo frowned, flipping through her large book. "I've never heard of anything like it before."

"We can't bleed," I pointed out, looking at my own hand. "We don't have any blood."

"Perhaps it's just a metaphor?" Cleo wondered. "Readings often come out that way."

"Maybe it's just talking about suffering," Rowley chimed in thoughtfully, "in a weird, gory kind of way."

"What makes the dead suffer?" Cleo asked, looking at Rowley.

"I don't know," Rowley shrugged. "Maybe being dead."

I remembered what that creepy Darla spirit had said at the hospital: *'Theys wants my blood!'* Her words didn't sound so crazy anymore. She'd mentioned blood and suffering, which was exactly what we had been talking about. At least that made a little more sense. I thought about what I had heard, trying to piece it all together.

"Cleo."

The two of them stopped talking, looking at me.

"What's the Reaper?"

"Like, the Grim Reaper?" Rowley asked.

"Not sure," I frowned, "just a Reaper. Is there anything in that book about a Reaper?"

"A Reaper?" Cleo repeated, thinking. "I might have heard something like that before." She flipped through her book, scanning page after page for some sort of information. "There's a short article I read about that from somewhere." She closed the book, going back to the endless shelves for a different copy. "It really didn't say much."

She brought out a different book, an older one with a grey, rotting cover. On the front it read, *Strange Happenings of the Eighteenth and Nineteenth Century*.

"What's that all about?" Rowley asked, leaning over my shoulder to see.

"I remember one chapter that mentioned something like that," Cleo repeated, flipping through the book. "They may have used another word though. Would there be another term for it?"

I thought about it. "Anything to do with ghost blood."

"DG," Rowley reminded me, "we're pretty blood-free beings on this side."

"I know," I replied, "but this has got to be connected."

"Here we are," Cleo smiled, setting the book on the table, "ghost master, phantom keeper— the Legend of the Immortal."

"A legend?" Rowley questioned. "I thought one of the perks of dying was a lack of all the history-learning stuff."

"Shut up." I rolled my eyes. "Let's hear it."

"There isn't much to hear," Cleo told me, looking up from the book. "It's only a few sentences."

"Read them anyway."

"Legend says," she began, "that there was once someone who sold their soul to the devil so he could live forever. He was reaped by the devil, so the people said. Therefore, he was known as The Reaper."

"Classic," Rowley snorted, leaning back. "Did they sign their name in blood?"

"I'd assume so," Cleo responded with sincerity. "The Legend says that because this person could not die, they could speak to ghosts."

"So that narrows it down to every psychic in the world, right?" I asked, leaning forward.

"Not exactly," Cleo explained. "They also used ghosts in the ritual."

"What ritual?"

Cleo closed her book. "The one required to live forever."

Chapter 17

"Immortality you say?" Clyde asked, looking up from his desk. After a few more minutes of talking I agreed to speak with him again. I didn't wanna keep bugging the guy, as it had been a few hours since our last visit. But as far as I knew he knew more about this sort of thing than I did. Besides, he had connections with other spirits. If there was anyone else who had heard of this before, it was him.

"Yeah, and the Reaper," Rowley asked, "Do you know anything?"

Clyde was silent for a moment, processing the information. I looked back at Alder. The guy had been in the room since we came back. He was silent, as usual.

"I've seen a lot since I began guiding other spirits," he began, folding his hands together. "But I usually try to stay out of anything that goes beyond purgatory."

"What about the other psychics?" Rowley asked. "The one's from before?"

Clyde was silent. I turned to Rowley. "What psychics?"

"We're not the only paranormal business in town, if you haven't already learned that," Alder cut in from his remote spot against the wall. "We've had some bad run-ins with these other psychics before."

"What kind of 'bad' do you mean?" I asked, turning to face him.

"Let's just say," Clyde finished, wheeling to face his friend, "that we are more careful about which spirits we take requests from now."

"Yeah," Rowley added. "If I didn't bring you in they'd kick you out."

"So are any of these 'bad guys' possibly the Reaper?" I frowned. This was all really vague, and I didn't like vague.

"Possibly," Clyde began again. "Let me show you something."

He stood up, walking over to a metal book shelf on the other side of the room. I waited with Rowley as he pulled out a thick, dilapidated binder with papers practically falling out. He brought it back to the desk, setting it down in front of us.

"This," he opened it to the front cover, "is a record of every paranormal client I've helped since I started assisting spirits."

"And when was that?" I asked, looking up at him.

"I'm not *that* old DG," he smiled. He gestured at the title, which showed a date from the early 2000's.

He flipped through a few pages, stopping near the beginning of the volume. He swung the book around, his fingers resting on top of an older photograph.

"This is Jonathan West, age thirty-three, 2001," Clyde informed with a tap on the photo. The man was smiling for the camera, sitting in an office quite different from this one. The room was much more worn and messy compared to Clyde's pristine space. It was taken a while ago, but the photo was still in good shape. The guy had dark brown hair and smiling green eyes, unashamed of having his photo taken.

"Is he dead?" I asked, touching the photo.

"He is now." Alder didn't sound too pleased.

"Yes," Clyde agreed, frowning at the memory. "One of the most powerful psychics I've met in the field."

I turned to Clyde, "What happened to him?"

"He had an obsession with power," Alder answered, stepping forward to the photo. "He did anything to strengthen his own psychic abilities."

"Is that the guy that had a business, like you?" Rowley asked, hanging over the three of us.

"Yes," Clyde replied. "He had a side job of helping wandering souls, much like my own. Unfortunately his help came with a price."

"What price?" I asked, staring at the man.

"He used spirits to make him stronger," Clyde explained, "like he owned them. Each spirit would be helped in exchanged for a favor. They would help him steal or launch schemes for extra cash. He used them until they were drained of their spirit."

"What happens then?" I asked, turning to him.

"They fade," he replied gravely. I thought about what Rowley said about fading, how spirits would pass on.

"How can you do that?" I frowned.

"By killing a ghost," Alder explained. I jumped, forgetting he was next to me. "It's rare, but it's possible."

"Not *kill*," Clyde cut in, alarmed by his comrade's harsh tone. "No, no. How do I explain this?" He glanced around the room. "Ghost can be 'gotten rid of' if you will. Everything on earth has energy yes? Ghosts too have some kind of energy. There's is just different from the living."

I nodded, following along.

"In a way, this energy can be harnessed. Ghosts use energy when they run or move objects. I'm not quite sure how much energy they have. I suppose it depends on the person. Perhaps a smarter man could use ghosts to power light bulbs," he smiled, "But to get back to the point, once all your energy is gone you would fade from purgatory. Simple as that."

"Still sounds painful," Rowley commented.

I looked back down at the picture. "So that's what this man did?"

"This man abused other spirits until they died," Clyde nodded. "A disgrace to mankind."

"But how did he die then?"

"He did the worst thing a living person could possibly do." Clyde explained. His anger had dropped. He was in a completely different mood now, solemn, withdrawn. "He tried to consume a spirit."

"They tooks it! They tooks my blood!"

The words from the howling spirit echoed in my mind. Even without a body I suddenly felt cold. I thought my death made me safe, protected me from any danger. But I was wrong.

"To consume a ghost is to take all its power, all its energy until there is nothing left," Clyde went on, oblivious to my shock. "It gives the consumer heightened psychic abilities, health and well-being. Some say it even gives the living extended life. John had used spirits' energy before, but not all at once. And of course, it's almost impossible to do."

"What happened then?" The words were drawn from my mouth, my eyes glued to the picture. The story sounded strange. It was like the odd, prickly feeling I got before I received a piece of memory. Was this part of a memory? Something I'd forgotten?

"He had all the proper equipment, which I've since destroyed." Clyde went back to his desk and sat down. "One night he captured a wayward spirit and locked himself with the ghost in his workspace. He told no one of the deal, not even his business partner."

I looked at Clyde. "You?"

He nodded. "I didn't want to partake in the ceremony. He had offered me half of the ghost's energy months before, but I turned him down. I thought he would have dropped the idea since then. I couldn't have been more wrong."

I felt Rowley shudder next to me, and I couldn't help but do the same.

"Fortunately, I had left something in my office and came back late that night. I had no idea what was going to happen that night, or how much pain it causes the victim."

"He saw it with his own eyes," Rowley interrupted, exaggerating with hand motions. It was then I realized he's probably heard this story before.

"So I was there with him in the office," Clyde continued with his eyes remaining downcast at the photograph below. "I was completely alone. West had a gun, he made me betray my morals. I was the one that held the spirit down."

I remembered Clyde could touch ghosts, that he could do so as long as Rowley could remember. Who knew that talent could have such a dark side?

"It was a tough fight. I even got a few bruises I didn't know could form."

"Tell him what happened next," Rowley cut in, eyes filled with the wonder of the story. "Tell him about the fight."

I frowned. "There was a fight?"

"Not like the action movies, but yes. When West first started the ceremony, the scream was awful. It made the spirit struggle like hell. I backed out. I couldn't take it any longer."

"So you got up and punched 'em!" Rowley exclaimed.

"Or something like that," Clyde smiled. "The spirit got loose, but I was focused on John. I managed to get a hold on another spirit to help me. It possessed West. I wasn't thinking, I just wanted him to stop. When I let the ghost free, I never thought it would—"

He paused, giving a moment of silence. "The captured ghost escaped. The other one wouldn't leave John. It made him shoot himself. I alone was the only witness, and I was helpless to stop him."

Clyde ended the tale, closing the book as he did. I thought about how big that book was, and all the clients Clyde had known through the years. Out of all those people, it seemed like John West was the only one that died.

"And now no one does anything like that anymore, right?" I asked, sounding a little more nervous than I meant.

"I thought that sort of activity stopped," Clyde frowned at me, "then you showed up."

I felt two pairs of eyes turn to me. Startled by the looks I realized how all this was connected. If whoever killed me was a psychic, they wouldn't want me sticking around as a ghost. But what if they wanted me here because they *planned* it, and the intention was to get rid of me?

"That bleeding ghost… that's the only thing that can explain those deaths."

"All these murders going on must be for a reason," Clyde started. "I'd guess serial killer, but all these deaths have had been deeply affecting the afterlife. There must be a connection."

"So you think I'm meant to be some sort of sacrifice?" I asked, thinking about what Cleo said.

"No, there has to be another motive," Clyde mumbled, folding his hands together in thought. "If you don't mind Rowley, I'd like to speak to DG alone."

Chapter 18

"So what is it?" I asked, turning back to Clyde. Rowley was gone. Alder was at the door, but his back was to us. He turned back at Clyde, a question on his lips.

"My 1:30 should be coming up now," Clyde said to Alder, cutting off whatever he was about to say. "Could you get his gift please?"

Alder seemed hesitated. I couldn't tell if it was because he wanted to stay or if he didn't want to be Clyde's secretary.

"Of course," he said curtly before he left. Now it was just me and the business man. He remained calmly seated at his desk, casually picking up his phone to type something on it.

"Do you believe in winning a business deal with bribery, DG?" Clyde asked me conversationally. He seemed tense from Alder's response.

"Um, no," I replied.

"I don't either," he agreed.

I doubt this was what he wanted to talk about. Clyde knew it too, so he went down to business.

"I apologize for having to make things so dramatic DG," Clyde began, still writing on his phone. "I just thought we were due for a little conversation. It feels like we barely know each other."

I remained where I was, not quite sure what to say. Being alone in a private room like this gave me the feeling I was in some sort of trouble.

"You can sit down if you want."

Realizing there was a chair right by his desk, I did.

Clyde looked up from his phone. "So, did you find anything interesting on your hunt for your body?"

Didn't we just talk about that? My answer came out in a stammer. "Rowley can tell you—"

"I want you to tell me DG," he insisted, using the same tone. "You're so quiet."

"Well, I swear, I don't know anything," I assured him. "Just what we've told you."

Clyde sighed, rubbed the surface of his laptop to life, and began typing on the keyboard. "I know you lied to me about your murder."

So that was what he wanted. I readjusted myself in my seat. "I'm sorry. It's just that I didn't know for sure, and I was confused by everything."

"You can save the excuses," he said. He kicked off the wall by his desk and rolled closer to me. "I'd rather know if there was anything else you've been keeping from me. It's your past, DG. I'd hate for you to never get your memories back due to your need to keep secrets."

I looked down into my lap. "If there was anything else you didn't know, I'd tell you."

"Good." He reached for a pen. "Your death seems to be a lot more than it appears to be. And you have to remember I've got my own safety to worry about." He clicked the pen and began to write. "If anything else comes up, you won't be afraid to tell me, right?"

I nodded. "I'll let you know."

"Good." He stopped writing. Clyde shook the pen a few times, followed by clicking it several times on the desk. "Stupid thing."

"Ok, can you please stop clicking that pen?"

I blinked. No one else in the room seemed to have spoken. Clyde certainly didn't notice.

"You can come in now," he called, a bit louder than he was talking before.

I looked behind me, wondering who he was talking to. "What?"

The door opened. An older man, a living man, hobbled into the room. I stepped out of the way as he went by, his cane almost stabbing my foot. I looked back at Clyde.

"Do you know where Rowley went?"

"You're just jealous because I created a new instrument."

My head felt funny. It was light and pounding and the whole room seemed lighter. I was having another flashback.

"Mr. Long, it's nice to see you!" Clyde smiled, getting up to help the man into his chair. He was ignoring me, I realized. Now that a customer was around of course he couldn't talk to me now. He'd seem crazy. And I certainly couldn't explain what was going on, not now. I did my best to slip out the door before it closed.

"Thanks," I managed as the light around me grew brighter.

"Glad I could help you today," Clyde smiled at the customer.

Chapter 19

I made it out just in time. I nearly crashed against the wall, sinking to my knees and holding my head in my hands. My whole body was shaky, and for the first time ever I felt out of breath.

"So are you going to tell her or what?"

It was that guy again. The guy with bulgy eyes was staring at me across the table. We were sitting at a table, the smell of baked goods telling me we were at some sort of eating establishment. The orange countertop and crazy lamp shades were familiar to me. It was the café, the one Cleo had taken me to.

There was a girl with us to. She was our age, calm blue eyes with caramel hair draping down her back. Here eyebrows were a different color than her hair, the same dull brown as her roots. They were knitted together in confusion.

"Tell me what?"

My hand ran through my hair and I looked out the window. I took a deep breath. *"I found out some new clues."*

The girl perked up. She rested her hands on the table, eyes gleaming. *"On the killer?"*

"Yeah, the guy," my friend told her. He had stopped clicking his pen and showed her the notes he had taken. *"The guy who's been killing all those people."*

"Or girl," she added. Her eyes flicked back to me. *"What did you find?"*

I glanced back down at my hands. *"There's a connection about the way each of them died. For each death, almost all of them took place in public. It's like the murderer doesn't care who sees him or not. And that's just the thing – nobody has."*

The girl lowered her eyes. *"You're talking about the dead again, aren't you?"*

I held my tongue. *"I don't see how there's another way."*

She shook her head. *"Do you hear yourself? Do you think that's really possible?"*

I shrugged my shoulders. I honestly didn't know. *"After what we saw, I think anything's possible."*

Just then, a phone went off. The girl swiped it off the table to check it. *"I gotta go. I told The Big C I'd meet her by three."* She looked at each of us before standing. *"Call me if you learn anything, ok?"*

Our response was typical. *"We will."*

As fast as it came on, the scene vanished. I jerked awake, the sight of Clyde's hallway scaring me half to death. I had to re-adjust to being dead again. I forgot I didn't know how to breathe.

After brushing myself off I stood up. Since we had become un-official partners in crime, I should probably go find Rowley. Nobody was around out in the hall, or at least no *body*. The man in black was rounding the corner as I peered down the hall. I walked over to him.

"Hey, have you seen Rowley?" I asked him.

Alder stopped to answer. "He thought you two would be a while," he replied. With his glasses, I honestly couldn't tell if he was looking at me or not. I could only assume he was. "He left."

"Where to?" I asked. Did he really expect me to find him in the middle of a big city? I don't think that guy thinks sometimes.

"Lincoln High School," he told me. The guy in front of me wasn't very expressive. He mostly kept the same tone with every word. I don't get what Clyde saw in him.

"Oh, ok." Alder didn't reply. I started to turn away from him. "Thanks." Still no reply. It occurred to me that in Clyde's story, he didn't give a name to the ghost. The one that made John West shoot himself.

"Hey Alder," I began again, turning back to him. "How did you meet Clyde?"

Alder seemed generally surprised by the question. "He's one of the few acquaintances I know that hasn't passed on. I began to help him with his business, and we've stuck together ever since."

I nodded, taking in the information. "How long have you been together then?"

"A long time," Alder said. With a second thought he added, "A very long time."

I remembered the way they acted in the office. It must be hard for Alder, spending all his time with a living person. It was a constant reminder of the things he could no longer do. I should probably get going, but there was still one more question on my mind.

"How'd you die?"

Alder was silent for a moment. Maybe he was wondering if I could handle the information.

"I was out alone, and there wasn't time for me to get medical attention," he finally said.

"For what?" I asked.

Alder stood still against the wall. He wasn't too expressive about these things. "The knife."

I must have looked confused. "What?"

He tapped his sunglasses. "The knife."

~

I didn't get to see directly what Alder was talking about, but I think I knew. Rowley told me how some ghosts move on after death, how their wounds clean up all by themselves. Some don't.

After a few hours of wandering I managed to find the high school. It took a while, but it was nice not to be bothered by the hot afternoon sun. Alder had told me to head north, close to Lincoln Park. Thankfully, without Rowley around I didn't have to worry about possible traffic. I was able to take a bus without flying out the end like he did.

I looked the building up and down. Could I have possibly gone to school here? I tried to call back any memories or past actions involving this place. Nothing came up immediately. Then again, nothing ever did.

Rowley had explained to me some time earlier it was the middle of August, so the school was closed. There wasn't any obvious way for me to get in. I settled for walking around the building, looking for any useful windows or doors that have helped me before. In the middle of a football field, a high school team practiced in the early afternoon. Passing the gate to the field, the team seemed fine. It seemed to me they hadn't just lost a valuable team member, which told me I hadn't been on the football team. I was ok with that.

I spotted someone on the bleachers, their bright yellow shirt sticking out from the dull silver seats like a hippo in a kiddy pool. Surprised, I ran up the steps.

"I guess you do never touch the ground," I commented, sitting next to Rowley.

Rowley was slouched, resting his head in his hands. He would've been sitting normally if he hadn't been floating a few inches above the ground. The side of his mouth was sagging to form a sort of frown. He looked a little spaced-out, pausing as if he didn't hear me at first. He must have been spaced out, that or watching the team.

"I don't sit," he said, eyes still looking out. "Sitting is for losers."

"Sure," I smirked, glancing out at the field. "What are you doing here?"

"Being bored," he floated up, turning to me. "Did Clyde send you here?"

"Not really," I frowned. "I think I'm up for doing a little research into my past."

Rowley crossed his legs in the air. "So this is your high school?"

I scanned the area again. "It might be."

He perked up, already floating down the steps a bit. "Need a tour?"

"If you mean a way in, then yeah." I got up, following. "How do you know your way around here?"

"Because I'm an expert in this town."

Chapter 20

Rowley showed me into the building via locker rooms left open for the practicing team. From there it was easy to get to the abandoned hallways and empty classrooms. I walked and Rowley hovered down the rows of lockers and tiled floors. Nothing felt familiar, but I wasn't going to give up.

"So, you seem to know you're way around?" I asked Rowley.

"Yeah," Rowley replied. "I already told you."

"No," I went on, "I mean, was this your high school?"

Rowley came to a halt, pulling up to an upright position.

"No," he sighed, waiting for me to catch up, "I didn't go to high school."

I bent an eyebrow, "You didn't?" Rowley looked fourteen or fifteen, definitely old enough for at least freshman year. "How'd that happen?"

"I had a sort of— delay," he shrugged, moving on again. I followed.

"What *kind* of delay?" I continued.

"The one where you're *dying*." Rowley rolled his eyes, spinning ahead and almost out of view. "They let you skip school when you're on your deathbed."

"Oh." I dragged behind, looking around the bulletin boards and painted walls. Nothing here pertained to me anymore, I wasn't a student. But did I go to school here? Did I once have friends, skip class down these halls? Did my murderer go here? In a few months, my forgotten friends would be starting school without me. It was a weird feeling. "Rowley, how'd you die?"

"What?" Rowley asked, pulling his head out of one of the lockers.

"How'd you die?" I asked again, looking at him. "Come on, I already told you mine."

"Well, you know," Rowley started, shifting in the air. He faced me to make sure he was in the best story telling position possible. "I was doing fine, living my life you know? Then one day I—" He paused, almost getting choked up. "One day I was stabbed."

My mouth fell open. "What?!"

"I'm kidding!" he laughed, flipping upside down to look at me. "Not everyone gets the dramatic murder routine."

My mind immediately went to Alder. I frowned, leaning against a locker. "Then seriously, how'd it happen?" I asked.

Rowley sighed. "It's no big deal."

"It's your *life*," I argued. "That's the biggest deal you can get."

He looked at me. "You really wanna know?"

I nodded. "Yes."

"Honest?"

"*Yes.* Get on with it."

Rowley paused, a sly look suddenly creeping on his face. His voice suddenly had a different tone to it.

"All right then, you asked for it."

I began to feel concern for my wellbeing. "What the hell are you—?"

Rowley kicked off the air and lunged at me. Before I could even figure out what was happening he grabbed me, his hands on my shoulders and my eyes practically staring up his nose. Then next thing I knew Rowley slammed his head inside mine. The school was gone. All sound was gone. The world went black.

~

Rowley was lying in the hospital bed— half asleep, half awake. What had it been now, two weeks? He didn't feel the least bit better than he had when he'd checked into this place. He would've preferred to stay at home, like before. But when someone calls an ambulance on you, you kind of have to stay in the hospital. Especially after fainting at the game like that. Now he couldn't play sports anymore. For two weeks he had been stuck in a sparse room with his bed and a reclining chair he wasn't allowed to sit in. His parents talked to doctors and his friends were barely allowed to see him. Now it was just him and the white walls.

They were really boring, those white walls. All they did was sit and stare at you all day, filling your mind with blank, empty, whiteness. On good days they gave Rowley a headache, and on bad days they started to close in on themselves. This did *not* make up for missing your best friend's soccer game, no matter how sick you were.

The door opened. Rowley did his best to sit up. An open door was usually the only action he got all day.

"Rowley?" someone asked. The door was barely open, just enough so Rowley couldn't see who it was. He tried to sit up more, but his body wasn't responding well.

"Yeah?" he croaked back. A hand went up to his throat. Did he really sound like that? It had been so long, he hadn't talked in a while. "Come in."

"Guys it's Rowley," the voice cried, pushing the door all the way open. All his friends, fresh from school, poured into the room. They all crowded around his bed, a *Get Well Soon* balloon in their midst.

"Hey," Stephen waved. "You're actually bald?" It was true. Rowley had lost his hair this week. It matched the pale skin and circles under his eyes. Maybe after this was all over, Rowley could be a model.

"You guys didn't have to run over here," Rowley beamed, his voice warming up.

"Well heck yeah I'm gonna go see my friend," Tristan replied, tying the balloon to his bed.

"Yeah, I mean, it's *cancer*. You could *die* tomorrow!" Stephen pointed out. Despite the setting medical jokes were taken lightly here. His friends were used to him being in and out of the hospital. A little too used to it, in Rowley's mind.

Rowley gave a short laugh. "Yeah."

Connie rolled her eyes. "You know they're just kidding, right?" The boys only smirked. Rowley tried to push the thought out of his head.

"What are you doing here— besides being at my death bed?"

"That's not funny!" Connie cut in.

Tristan beamed at the girl. He loved when his jokes caused a reaction. "We had to babysit a little hobo for you. The kid was begging us to see you."

"Rowley!" a familiar voice called from the back. A little boy, about five years old pushed through the crowd of friends. He scrambled to the front and jumped up onto the bed. He landed right on Rowley's foot, which kind of hurt like hell but Rowley didn't really care.

"Hey Will," he smiled, trying his best not to look like crap. He tried to sit up a little more, while his little brother leaned forward.

"The others said— they kept telling me— are you coming home yet?" the boy babbled.

Rowley sighed, using his arms to push himself up. "You know what mom and dad said. I have to wait until the cancer goes away."

"Or—" Tristan was cut off by an elbow from Connie.

"But when will you get better?" Will persisted, leaning closer.

Rowley reached out, ruffling his brother's hair. "Soon little buddy, I promise."

Will closed his eyes and grinned, swatting away Rowley hand. "But you said that last month."

Rowley's paused. It took him a while before he could answer. "I— yeah. I did."

He did say that last month, and the one before that. He thought he would be better by then.

"I got you a present," Will went on, fumbling for his backpack. Rowley smiled. Had it really been two months? Two and a half, if you counted the time he had to switch rooms. Will was getting taller. He could swear Will was taller. How did that happened in two months?

"Oh yeah? Whatcha got?" he asked.

"Mom let me buy it for you," he explained, pulling out a small bag. "Cause you lost all your hair."

"I want pictures of your head, by the way," Stephen cut in.

Rowley looked up at them. "Don't you have a trophy to rub in someone's face?"

Tristan held up his hands. "Relax, we just came to drop him off." Already he and Stephen were starting to back toward the door. "But seriously, feel better man. We'll need you at the championships in a few months."

"I'll try," Rowley replied. "Make some decent passes for once, alright?"

"You know I won't!"

They were gone, leaving just Connie and Will. She came up to the side of the bed, resting her hand on and headboard. "We're coming in all day tomorrow, and we're bringing the others," Connie reminded him. "Get better, ok?"

"You betcha!" Rowley did his best to flash a winning smile. It must have worked, because she smiled back. He gave a final wave as she turned toward the door. It was always a bit sad, watching his friends leave. But soon, hopefully, he'd be able to walk out of this place himself.

"Now open it!" his brother insisted. Will slammed his hands on the bed as he spoke, giving Rowley another wave of accidental pain. He gritted his teeth and ignored it, adjusting himself to hold the present.

It wasn't a complex package, just a bag stuffed with cheap wrapping paper. Even with the paper, he could already make out the red color visible under the wrapping. It took no time at all for Rowley to tare out the thin sheets separating him from his brother's gift. Now, sitting on his lap was a bright red beanie. It was soft, the color vibrant against the dull white of everything else in the room.

Will was searching his brother's face with bright eyes, "You'll wear it, right?"

Rowley picked up the hat, examining it. "Heck yeah! Thanks little buddy."

Will crawled up to his brother's side. "You're gonna get better, right Rowley?"

Rowley hesitated. It never crossed his mind that he *wouldn't* get better. Of course he'd get better. But now that the question stared him in the face, Rowley wasn't so sure.

"Of course I will."

There was a sinking feeling in his stomach, or maybe that was cancer.

Will didn't seem convinced. He did that when he was upset, make you promise things over and over. But that didn't always mean it'd come true. "And you'll come home, right?"

It's bad to lie to children.

"Yeah."

"And teach me how to play football?"

"I will."

His brother watched intently, eyes locked on him. "Promise?"

Rowley watched his brother. Though having visitors usually cheered him up, he wasn't feeling so hot anymore.

"I promise."

Chapter 21

Rowley let go of me, pushing himself back and hovering a few feet away from me. His eyes were locked onto mine, scanning to read my reaction. I blinked, reality rushing back at me so suddenly it took me a few minutes for it to sink in.

"So," Rowley said, breaking the silence, "that's basically it." He drifted back even further, turning his head to look at some art projects on the wall.

"What was it?" I asked, going after him. He had cancer. I knew that. But a lot of people had cancer, there were so many types. And besides all that, I didn't see the actual day he died.

"It was leukemia," Rowley said, his voice seeming far away.

"Leukemia?" I repeated, stepping up to him. "That's what killed you?"

"It was more than that," he went on, his expression vacant. "It took longer, a couple more months, but yup," he nodded his head once, "it killed me."

"I'm sorry about that," I said, coming to his side. "That must have been hard on your friends, and your brother."

"Yeah," Rowley floated away, looking up at the ceiling. "It's all right though. They've recovered and stuff."

He floated up to a sign, using his finger to help him read it.

"Hey, here's the honor role. Were you smart?"

"How long has it been?" I asked, continuing to follow him, "since— you know."

Rowley tilted his head to the side. "I don't know." He shrugged it off, floating around the room. "A bit I guess. They're over it now."

"I get that," I replied, still deep in thought. "But why'd you show me that? Why not your death? Isn't that more self-explanatory?"

"I don't remember my death," Rowley explained as we rounded another corner.

"What?"

"I honestly don't remember," Rowley scratched his head. "I might have been asleep for the whole thing."

"That must be nice," I sighed, the memory of a knife wound flickering through my system.

"Besides, that's the thing about memories," Rowley went on. "You tend to forget the bad stuff. It doesn't do you any good to remember it."

I thought about Darla, that crazy spirit who was stuck on her memory about blood—whatever that was. She only thought of the bad stuff. Ghosts were a little clingy, sticking to their memories and living possessions. Rowley was one of the only ones with some sense, being a free spirit and all (no pun intended). Then again, the idea of forgetting the past kind of scared me. Especially when I spent the week trying to find it.

"Then what did you do after you died?" I asked, taking the lead, "when you were a new ghost, like me."

Rowley's face did a half-frown, more pensive than sad. "That was when I focused on the bad stuff."

"Oh." I had a feeling I wasn't going to get any more comments on that.

"If I didn't run into Clyde I'd still be in my old room right now," Rowley chuckled, though he wasn't smiling. "It took me months before I finally left home."

"And Clyde helped you?" We arrived at a new billboard with photos from the recent yearbook. I ran a finger through each picture, scanning for my face.

"I guess. He was just someone to talk to, really. None of the other ghosts like to talk to newbies. He showed me how to get by, how to carry on after your funeral." Rowley floated to my side and started at the top of the bill board while I searched the bottom. "Trust me, DG. After all this is over you should forget your life. It doesn't have anything to offer you."

I finished one of the pictures and looked up at him. "What about purgatory? What about doing that one thing to pass on?"

Rowley kept his eyes on the paper. "I missed my chance."

I blinked. "Missed your chance?"

"It doesn't matter." Rowley was raising his voice now. He crossed his arms and floating higher up toward the ceiling. He stopped near one of the top pictures, pretending to study it with a hand going through the glass to touch the photo. "Look, the point is after all this you won't need your memories anymore."

I tuned him out, scanning frame after frame. There had to be something here, there just had to.

"Toss 'em, forget 'em, sell 'em, I don't know. It's just not important."

I ran my finger against one of the top photos, my eyes catching sight of something.

"It's the best you can do when you're six feet under and they never even notice after—"

"Rowley," I cut off, staring at the picture. "It's me."

It was me – the real, breathing me. I was sitting at a table with two other students, listening to the boy next to me. I was in a different jacket. Those other clothes were probably in a drawer somewhere in this city, untouched. I was smiling, actually smiling with this other guy during a conversation that I didn't remember. But it had happened.

There were three of us alone at a table near the back. We didn't seem to mind though. There was me, sitting on the far left with my hands on the table, the way I sometimes sat in Clyde's office. In the middle was a girl, a girl with caramel hair laughing at some joke I probably would've liked too. Next to her a guy with bright hazel eyes was telling the story. His face was caught in the middle of a sentence, his hands gesturing to help explain the tale.

This was me. This was that part of my life that was taken away, stolen by death. I touched the glass, wishing I could reach through like Rowley and take the picture. I had eaten in that lunchroom, I had walked around this whole building. I turned, suddenly seeing the school in a different light. This was my high school.

And what was better, was that I knew the people.

"DG?" Rowley glanced down, noticing me for the first time. "You ok?"

"I know them." I pointed to the two kids in the photo. They had been in my memories, both of them. "This is my school Rowley. I went here. My friends went here."

"Oh," Rowley floated down. "That's great."

"I know the kids in this picture," I smiled, tapping my finger against the glass. "I've seen them in my flashbacks."

I traced my finger in a large circle over the shot. "If we find out about them, we may find out about me."

Rowley leaned in toward the photo. "Maybe. How do you know these people were that close? The yearbook could have messed around or something."

"Maybe, but it's something."

I scanned the pictures again. Not for me, but for the other people in the picture. There had to be something, a name, maybe an interview. "Here!"

It was the girl again. There was no sign of the boy or myself, but she was standing with a large group of people, all wearing the same t-shirt.

"Literature Society," Rowley read from the photo, coming to hover beside me. "You sure have interesting friends."

"There's a list of names on the side," I pointed out, stepping to read the names more clearly. They were listed in a row according to where the person was standing— it was perfect! If I couldn't find my own name, at least I'd have someone else's.

"Sarah Conwell."

Did you hide the book yet?

I blinked, the sudden voice catching me off guard. The last memories I'd seen were Rowley's, so I had forgotten mine were still lingering around too.

"Conwell?" Rowley jerked his head to look.

400 S. State Street.

"What?" I asked, not listening. It had been a girl's voice— Sarah's?

"Her name's Sarah Conwell?"

"Yeah, is that someone you know?" I turned to look at him.

"No," Rowley frowned at the picture. "I've never seen the girl before."

"Still," I smiled at Rowley, "we should find her, today. We can get someone to talk to her, communicate with her. She might know something."

"Today? We'd have to find her first."

"Today, tomorrow, it doesn't matter." I turned and bolted down the hall, toward the exit of the building.

"We don't even know where she is. How are you going to find her?"

"I got a clue."

Rowley cocked his head. "What clue?"

I grinned. "400 South State Street."

Chapter 22

Harrison

Alder's hands were on the edge of the desk. He leaned forward, staring into the face of an unaware Clyde Harrison. "I don't want you to help him."

A startled Clyde looked up from his work. "What's this?" Straightening his glasses, he blinked at the unexpected appearance of his friend. With a quick cough he managed to collected himself. "It's a little too late for any of that."

"You know it isn't," Alder told him. He relinquished the desk and crossed his arms. "There's still time to drop out. Let the damn kid fend for himself."

Clyde watched. He knew Alder hated when Clyde dealt with the other spirits, especially the younger ones. They didn't always correlate with his ideas. "To back out now would be rather harsh, not to mention rude." He went back to his work, taking his eyes off the ghost. "Besides, Rowley has such a high opinion of the boy. I have to help him."

"You never 'have' to do anything." Alder was quite stern about this. "You never 'have' to take any of these cases. You never 'had' to become involved with the dead." He stopped, meeting Clyde's eyes. "You can't go through with this one. This isn't something to take lightly."

"Maybe for you it isn't." Clyde looked back at Alder, a new curiosity in his eyes. "What made you change your mind?"

Alder remained where he was, his tone rigid. "I think we need to stop this. All of it."

Clyde scowled, leaning back in his chair. He hated when people told him what to do. "End my communications? That's a no Alder, you know I can't. I'm not going to ignore the dead. I've known some of them for years. It'd be idiotic to walk out now."

"They're better off on their own."

Clyde smirked. "I highly doubt that."

Now it was Alder's turn to scowl. "Well you wouldn't know."

"Now Alder," Clyde started, "I don't know what you do in your free time, but you seem to constantly complain about mine. You have to allow me to make my own choices. I'm not like you. I'm a living person and I have needs to fulfill."

"Not at the expense of others."

Clyde frowned, "At whose expense? I'm not doing anything they don't agree to."

Alder fell silent. Clyde leaned back and eyed him. The ghost was giving him a threatening glare.

"Don't mock death, Harrison."

Clyde sneered. "You're the one that wants to live again," he chided. "Perhaps it's you who's doing the mocking."

Alder recoiled, "If there was anywhere else I could go, I'd leave."

"But you can't," Clyde mimicked from past conversations, getting up. "Where would you go? Everyone else you know has gone on. Everyone but me."

Alder remained stiff. He didn't need his own story thrown back into his face.

"You agreed to help me with the departed, and I agreed to help you."

"That was a lifetime ago," Alder argued. Time seemed to travel much slower for the dead than for the living.

"Think you've found something better then?" he asked. "Think you've found a new way out? Think you're better than the other ghosts? Scared the Reaper will turn you down?" Alder had nothing to say to this.

Exasperated, Clyde went back to working at his desk. "Make all the deals you want. Drink a thousand gallons of blood. I already told you, I can't help you with any of that and I won't. You're stuck the way you are."

Alder opened his mouth to rebuke him, then closed it.

"Well speak up!" Clyde demanded. "Don't give me the silent treatment."

"I," Alder started, "I can't work with this one. This boy, DG, I can't let myself do this."

"Why?" Clyde persisted. "What's there to be guilty about?"

Alder didn't say anything.

Clyde snorted. "No matter. Nothing can be done about it now." Without looking at the spirit he sighed and snatched the paper and pen he was using before. He began to write, while Alder turned to leave. Once again the ghost was invisible to the world.

"I'm going to do what I have to for our young DG," Clyde continued, not caring if Alder listened. "Whether you like it or not."

Chapter 23

DG

"400 South State Street, what *is* that?" Rowley asked, zooming to catch up with me for once. We had hit the streets. The city was in full swing as I wove in and out of various crowds and sped through traffic lights.

It was funny to run without all the sweat and fatigue, but it wasn't something I could do forever. I didn't have a body or muscles to get sore, but I could feel my – I don't know what you'd call it – my energy drain the longer I ran. I knew I couldn't go on for much longer, so I slowed to a walk to let Rowley catch up.

"I don't know," I replied. "But I'm going to find out."

"You're really going to hunt these people down, aren't you?" Rowley smirked as he caught up to me.

"Yeah, I am," I replied, looking ahead. "It's all I have. Do you have a problem with that?"

"What, me? No, why would I?" Rowley frowned, lying on his back to look at me.

"You're acting like you don't want this to get anywhere," I frowned, still not looking at him.

"Hey," Rowley said back, offended, "you're the one going off on crazy hunts ever since you died. I'd be more supportive if you didn't keep making it so hard." He stuck his tongue out at me.

"Hey, just because you left your family doesn't mean I'm going to leave mine."

"What?" Rowley sat up in front of me, making me come to a halt. "Hey, hold on there. I did *not* leave my family."

"You said so yourself: 'forget them. They're better off without you,' remember?" I started walking again. "I can't do that, Rowley. I have to know."

"I didn't say it like that!"

"Yes you did."

"Then I didn't mean it," he rolled his eyes. "I'm just saying you might want to think about—"

"Oh hello."

I almost ran into the figure, turning at the last second so the girl wouldn't trip. I turned to find Cleo standing at my side, looking at me with mild surprise. She was wearing another ridiculous outfit, another thrift shop dress and a bandana featuring various dancing goats on it.

"Hello DG," she smiled at me, "Rowley. How is your search?"

"Oh hey Cleo," Rowley half smiled, straightening up. He wasn't going to argue in front of company.

"Hi," I stepped around and let her continue walking at my side. "It's all been interesting."

"Searches often are," she replied, stopping at the light. I pulled up short, almost forgetting regular people couldn't walk across traffic. "Have you found anything?"

"Well, actually," I started. Rowley rolled his eyes. "Do you know a Sarah Conwell?"

"Sarah Conwell?" Cleo repeated, blinking at the name. "No, I'm sorry. How long has she been dead?"

"No, not like that," I cut in. "She's a *living* person. Do you go to high school with her?"

"Oh, no. I'm homeschooled," Cleo blushed. "It's much easier to study the telepathic and transparent arts that way."

"Right," Rowley nodded.

"Anyway, I'll keep a lookout for any person like that," Cleo continued. "Does she travel around town much?"

"No," I said, thinking back to the picture, "but she might be with a guy, maybe."

I thought about the two of them in my memories when it suddenly clicked. The girl's voice, Sarah's, had been familiar. The two teens from the hospital, it had to be them. What had she called the boy? Ricardo?

"She's definitely with a guy," I said again, drawn back into reality. "If you see them, let me know." I started backing away from her. "I'm really sorry but I have to keep moving."

"Yup." Rowley told her. His normally friendly tone was becoming a bit salty. "To be honest I'm not even sure where we're going. But it's super important we get there."

I rolled my eyes. "You don't have to come. Stay with Cleo if you want."

"I'll come," Cleo cut in, turning to face me. "I wasn't heading anywhere important anyway."

"No, it's fine." The only thing I was thinking about was getting to 400 South State Street as fast as possible. These memories had always felt rather personal to me, something private. I didn't want either of them to come along.

"But where ever you're going, it might be wise to have a living person with you," Cleo pointed out. "You can't talk to this Sarah on your own."

"Alright," I reasoned, stepping back to join them, "if you really want to."

"Actually, I can't," Rowley said, coming up to my side. "I've got other things to do."

"What?"

"As much as I love these crazy hunts," he started, a bit of backtalk creeping into his voice, "I've got things I have to do on Fridays."

I frowned. "Fine, if that suits you."

"Yeah, it does." He gave us one last look, "See ya." He flew off, leaving me and Cleo standing there.

"You have an odd friend there," Cleo smiled.

"He has his quirks," I decided. "Let's go."

Chapter 24

"What do you need a library for, DG?" Cleo asked as we stood before the building. "I didn't think the dead had much use of books."

I knew I was searching for a book, but I didn't think I'd end up at a library. We both were standing at the bottom of a tall red building, complete with mini archways and a row of flags along the side. Four stone owls were carved into the corners of the green rooftops, which jutted out to the sides and seemed to be surrounded by green fire. If I hadn't been trying to discover my past I might have taken time to enjoy the architecture.

"It's not that," I started. Most of my recovered memories seemed to have been helping me. It's like every time I got close to something, a memory would kick in to clear the path. That girl's voice had been talking about a book. If I wanted to find Sarah or that other guy, it must have something to do with this book. I glanced down the street, where people had, and still were, giving Cleo odd looks the entire trip here. I sighed. "I'm sorry, can you at least pretend you're not talking to thin air?"

"But I thought it was better to let others see the truth," Cleo replied, frowning.

"We don't have time to explain everything to everyone," I explained, a bit exasperated. "Just do it?"

"All right," Cleo replied. She reached for something in her pocket, "if it will make you happy." She pulled out her phone, holding it up to her ear. "Is this ok?"

She was still looking at me, but at least she looked normal to the outside world.

"That's fine," I replied, turning. "Let's go in." I started explaining what had happened beforehand, how the voice I'd been hearing led me to this point. Cleo was probably the only one I wouldn't mind explaining this to, since she seemed pretty accepting about anything I told her. Maybe in her psychic mind, she knew it was the truth. Or maybe she was crazy. I really didn't know.

The library was pretty big. I might have passed it a few times on my ways through the city, but I never took the time to really look at it until now. The high ceilings and multiple levels gave off a feeling I could've spent my life in here and not finish all of the books. I followed Cleo in, gawking as I did.

"What book are you looking for, DG?" she asked, glancing back at me. "I can look it up on one of the computers."

I looked at her. "Well, I kind of I don't know."

She didn't seem too fazed. "Then do you know which section it's in?"

I broke eye contact. "No."

"Which level?"

"No."

"Do you know what we're even looking for?"

"Well, no." Embarrassment wasn't something you needed a body to feel. "Sorry."

Luckily I was with someone who wasn't easily frustrated. "I guess we'll have to start from scratch then," she decided.

"I know." I headed into the lobby of the library. Surprisingly there were no books in this area for me to search. "It's a hidden book, so it's got to be somewhere out of the way. It's definitely not checked out, so it's somewhere where an average person wouldn't find it." I could only think of the miles of books to come. "It might take a while."

"There's fiction on the second floor," Cleo explained, pointing up the stairs. "That's where I usually go. It would be a good place to hide any sort of strange book." Considering the kinds of books Cleo had in her room, I guessed her suggested section would be a good place to start. We headed up the stairs.

I reached the top before her. Thousands of books among dozens of bookshelves were scattered about, and this was only the first floor. Although books seemed to take up the majority of the space the library seemed to have a flare for art as well. The decor included some older paintings and a miniature replica of the bean.

Cleo gave the room an once-over. "If it's hidden, I suppose the computers won't be any help." She turned to me. "Who hid it?"

"I uh," I hesitated. "I think it was someone I knew. Someone close to me."

Her face brightened. "Well, where would you hide a book?"

I looked back. "What?"

"One of your friends hid the book, and friends think alike," she pointed out. "Where would you hide it?"

"Ma'am, could you please turn off your cell phone?" A librarian asked from the counter. "They aren't allowed to be used in the building."

Cleo obliged. Thinking it over, I turned toward the mountain of bookshelves.

"I'd hide it away from all these people."

There were over eight levels in the entire building. Since Cleo brought me here, I trusted this was the strangest section. I figured that was good as any place to start, but this room was just as big as the ground floor. Cleo seemed to know her way around, so I followed her.

"There are two sections on this floor, the left and right of the stairs," I noticed as I trailed behind. "I'll check over here. You can look on the other side. It'll be faster that way."

"Ok," she nodded, going to the right. I turned the other way. One of the perks of being dead was that no one would notice me here. I could look anywhere I wanted and no one would object. Curious, I ran through the aisles of book shelves, waiting to see if any caught my fancy. Nothing did. I went to the set of tables were various people were reading. Smiling to myself, I stepped up onto one of tables, standing on top.

"Does anyone know where I can find a hidden book?" I asked, a little louder than my normal voice. No one looked up. I guess no ghosts were in the library either. My smile broadened, as I crouched down in front of one of the readers. "Can you help me?"

"SHHH!"

I turned, thinking Cleo had come back. Instead a small twig-like figure was zooming toward me, his legs crossed and a finger smushed against his lips. He didn't stop until he was right against my face, his wagging finger bumping into my nose.

"SHHH!"

"Hey, ok, I'm sorry," I snapped, backing away from the figure. "They can't even here me."

"No shouting in the library," the figure insisted, ignoring my words. "No standing on the table. And most importantly of all, no disturbing the reader!"

"I was just playing around," I insisted, hopping onto the floor.

"No playing in Lyly Berry's library," the ghost Lyly pressed on. He zoomed back a few feet above my head. "You mustn't break the rules."

He was a very short man, his legs tightly crossed and a hand resting on each knee. His face was pinched, with squinty eyes and a long nose over a thinly-pressed mouth. His short fading hair emanated from a shiny bald spot on his head, and his rectangular glasses were inching off the edge of his nose. He was dressed in a suit. It dawned on me he must have been a librarian.

"Ok, ok," I apologized, holding up my hands, "I'm sorry."

"Old friends mustn't break the rules," he said again, hovering off to the other side of the room. "It isn't proper."

Friend? I've been called worse. That proved that I must have been in this place before. I turned, going back toward the book shelves. To my right there was a sign on the top of the shelf read: *Historical Nonfiction*. I was searching for facts about my past, right? It was as good a place as any to start.

I walked by, looking down the rows and rows of shelves. At the end of one of the rows a large stone gargoyle perched on a stone slab, hunched to strike with one claw curled in attack. It looked like a winged-panther with feathers. It had plumage sticking out from each paw, no tail, and a big cat face snarled in an angry grimace. But the way it looked, the way its mouth arched up from its nose, it almost—

"It looks like he has a mustache."

"SHH!"

The all-too-familiar shush from a librarian made me flinch. The memory was fuzzy, but the other voice was one I had recognized from earlier. I had heard it before. Maybe I had passed them in the city at one point.

Curious, I continued down the hallway. The gargoyle seemed to stare at me through its vacant, stone eyes. As I neared the figure, I noticed a sign above the statue's head. It was a single arrow, a little red arrow pointing to the right. At the end of the row, I peeked around the corner.

Without warning a figure emerged from the bookshelves. I jumped only for a moment before remembering there were other ghosts in this library. The man turned toward me, unseen eyes scanning my shocked face.

"Alder?" I cried. Catching myself, I lowered my voice for the sake of Lyly. "What are you doing here?"

Alder calmly made his way toward me. "I could ask the same of you," he replied. He lifted his chin in the direction of Cleo. She was all the way at the end of the library, searching through rows of shelves. "I didn't know you had an interest in books."

"I'm working on my history," I replied.

"Of course," Alder replied in agreement. Yet his tone said otherwise. "You haven't seen Rowley around, have you?"

"Rowley? No, he said he had to go somewhere." I glanced back at Cleo. She had disappeared from Alder's view. "I assumed he was with you."

"I see," Alder replied. There was a pause in the conversation.

"Yeah," I nodded, "so, I really should be going."

"DG," Alder interrupted, "I hope you don't mind my prying. But I must ask. You wouldn't happen to be doing research on the Reaper, would you?"

I was almost too shocked to say anything. "Well, kind of. It came up with some of our research. Research on my death, that is."

Alder didn't seem satisfied with that answer. "Are you or are you not trying to research the Reaper?"

I frowned. "What if I am?"

"Drop it," Alder said simply. "You have no idea what you're getting yourself into."

"Your boss already gave me this talk," I started, turning away.

"Clyde doesn't know about this conversation," Alder informed, stepping around to face me, "and he's not going to find out."

My forehead creased. "Then why bother asking me all this?"

"For your own good," he answered. "Sooner or later, every new ghost learns of the Reaper. I'm here to tell you to quit while you're ahead."

For some reason, I suddenly thought of Alder's eyes. Who could've done something like that to him? Could someone have killed him for meddling in Reaper affairs?

Just like someone killed me?

"Alder, if you know something about my death or the Reaper," I began to ask him, "I'd love to know."

Alder didn't say anything. Finally, he spoke. "I've seen John West. I've seen what can happen to the dead," Alder explained. "I'm just trying to do what's right."

I shook my head. "If there is someone like the Reaper out there, stopping him is what's right."

Alder looked as if what I said had been very, very wrong. "Not when it's already too late."

I suddenly thought of Cleo. Maybe it was too late for Alder and me, but not for her. If she continued to help us, she could be in real danger. After all, she was very, very mortal.

Alder turned and began heading for the wall. "I hope you think about that."

And he was gone.

Chapter 25

I came back around toward the main reading area. Alder was nowhere to be found. I wouldn't be surprised if he had gone through one of the walls. What had he been doing here? Was he really here on his own business, or had he come to seek me out?

"DG?"

I snapped around to see Cleo, staring at me with her easy expression and clutching a book in her hands. "Are you all right?"

"Besides getting yelled at by the flying munchkin man, I'm fine." I caught myself. "Do you think that's the book?"

"No, it's something for me," she replied. "I knew the library was haunted, but I thought you were going to make friends."

Well, that would have bene something to mention to me before coming in.

"I think I found a good place though. Come and see." Cleo turned and motioned for me to follow. I glanced around as I did. Everyone else in the room seemed to be so absorbed in their books they missed the tie-dye girl walking around talking to herself. I was never one to be fascinated by books, but thank God for reading.

"I've been thinking," I started as I followed Cleo between two bookshelves, "it's a little weird to hide a library book in the library. Why not just check it out?"

"That's the thing," Cleo replied, stopping at the end of the row, "I don't think it's a library book."

I didn't follow. "How do you know that?"

Cleo didn't respond, but pointed toward the ceiling. "Because it's up there."

I looked up, and there indeed was a book. But it was entangled in the arms of a dinosaur. A pterodactyl hung from the ceiling with a book was nestled between its two outstretched arms. The way it was positioned made it look as if the dinosaur was reading. It had to be at least ten feet from the tops of the bookshelf, much less from our heads.

"Cleo." I couldn't take my eyes away from the book. "I don't think that's it."

"It's the right book," she replied, looking up as well. "I know it is."

I looked back at her. "How?"

"I do more than see the dead, remember?" she smiled at me. I half-smiled back. I remembered her psychic powers seemed odd at first as well, so I guess I trusted her on this one. But if that really was the book, it sure was in a tricky spot.

"How do we get it down?"

"That I'm not sure." She frowned, observing the book that seemed miles away. "How would you get it down?"

"Um, I can't fly," I pointed out. "If I was some crazy mutant I could probably do it."

"SHHH!"

We both turned to see Lyly again, perched on top of the bookshelf. "Keep your voices down in the library," he chided with a wagging his finger. "Don't disturb the readers."

"I'm sorry," Cleo apologized. "I must have forgotten my manners. I'm Cleo."

"SHHHHHHH!" Lyly hushed, diving down to Cleo's face.

"Sorry," Cleo whispered, just audible enough for the three of us to hear. "But we could really use some assistance sir. Could you help us with a favor?"

"Favor?" Lyly repeated, floating back to look at us both. "Does my old friend need a favor?"

"Um, yes," I confirmed, looking at him. "Could you get that book for us?"

I pointed upwards and Lyly's eyes followed. I braced myself for more shushing, going on about disturbance of library property and how we should shut up and all that. This was a bad idea.

"My old friend wants to read a book *now*?" Lyly asked, his face lighting up. "Lyly always helps readers get their books. That's what Lyly is here for!" He flew up to the pterodactyl, plucking the book from his grasps. "Put it back when you're done now."

"We might need help with that, but we will," Cleo smiled, still whispering. "Thank you."

Lyly nodded. "It's what I live for."

~

"*Ancient and Odd Tales of the Paranormal*," Cleo read, setting the book down on a table. "What exactly is this book supposed to have?"

"I don't really know," I replied, sitting down in the empty chair next to her. "I'm guessing it has something to do with the dead?"

"On page 887?" she asked, turning to me.

I raised my eyebrows. "You're a pretty good psychic."

"No. It says so right there." Cleo pointed at the index. It was truly an ancient book, with torn pages falling from the binding and pencil marks all over the place. But in the index one of the titles, *Tales from the Grave,* was circled with a pencil. Though the start of the section was on a different page, the number 887 was written clearly next to the text.

"It's worth a try," I shrugged, motioning for Cleo to flip to the page. We didn't know who wrote that, but as far as I knew it could have been Sarah or the guy she was with.

The page was the start of another story. A big title read, *The Tale of the Reaper*, in skinny wiggly letters. It looked almost like a too-cheesy ghost story to have any real fact, but we couldn't have come all this way for nothing.

"It looks like we're in the right spot," Cleo noted with a tap on the title.

"Yeah," I replied. Like the index, these pages were covered in highlights and underlined words. It looked like some margin-noted newspaper article. There were even comments written on the sides of the pages. While some read "this sounds stupid," others seemed to have more value. One of them near the middle of the story read "Read this part, important! How would the Reaper—"

"Use the spirits to live forever?" Rico asked.

It was the boy from before. Rico, the name Sarah had used at the hospital. Even though I hadn't seen him that night, I knew his voice. He was the boy I had seen earlier in the picture at the high school, the one telling the joke.

In the flashback, I was sitting in the library, one breath taken in after the other, sitting across from Rico. I was alive. I was there. The room seemed to be filled with an odd, wavy light like a dream. But I knew what I saw was real. I wasn't just hearing the memory this time, I was in it. Rico was sitting across on the other chair, leaning over to read the book facing me.

"I mean, he sold his soul for it. It'd have to be something freaky like that."

"It doesn't say," I replied, finishing the last sentence. *"All it talks about is the use of spirits."*

"Fresh spirits," Rico corrected, smirking.

"Do you think the Reaper is the one that murdered those people on the news?" I asked.

That was crazy. How did I believe that some guy from a story was responsible for killing people in real life? Why would such normal happenings need an abnormal explanation?

"That's what Mr. West thinks," Rico shrugged.

I turned back to the book. "And now we know why."

Sarah wasn't in this memory. If she hadn't been there, did she not know anything about this? I had to find out when I found her.

"Hey," Rico said, perking up, *"they say that banshees, those crazy spirits of the night, haunt the spots where the ritual occurred."*

I looked up at Rico. "And I think we know where that is."

Rico smiled back, an action that must have been shared many times in my life.

"Then we should probably go," I decided, shutting the book. "But we can't take this with us. Where do we hide it this time?"

I was confused, until I realized I was talking about the book. If that was the case, we must have been hiding it in multiple places, storing it from place to place. Why did we do that?

"Maybe in a place where it will blend in," Rico suggested, gesturing at the library. "Wherever in the world would there be a place like that?" he added with sarcasm.

"Fine," I replied, "but we can't have people trying to check it out. Where do we put it?"

Rico looked around, his eyes slowly moving toward the floating dinosaur. "I have an idea."

In a flash, I was back with Cleo, in the library, the *current* library. Everything was still, the readers reading and the two of us sitting. I felt stiff, the old memory of breathing making it awkward to be dead again.

"It says here that," Cleo started before glancing my way. "DG?"

"Cleo," I said, still recovering from the shock, "put the book away."

"Put the book away?" she repeated, lifting her eyebrows. "We just got it."

"I know, but I remembered," I told her, running a hand over the aging pages. "I know what it says and I know where we have to go."

"You have your memory back?" she asked, smiling.

"Bits and pieces," I shrugged. "I'll explain on the way. Get the book to Lyly, let's go."

I stood up, itching to be on the way. There was only one ghost I knew who was crazy enough to possibly know something. And I knew where to find her.

Chapter 26

All hunting aside, I had learned something else about myself. I may or may not have been a traitor. Rico had mentioned Mr. West, John West. He had when he broke into the hospital, and he had in my memory. John West had died many years ago, so how could he know him? Or, say West was really dead, and the two of us were finishing his work. Why would we do that?

"So you were involved in this kind of research even before you died," Cleo nodded, understanding my summary of my vision.

"Yeah," I replied. "But I guess we didn't see how real it all was."

"And you said you knew about Mr. West, the enemy of your current friends?" she added.

"Yeah," I affirmed. "I guess I'm still a little confused about that part."

Cleo was frowning. "DG, how long have you been having these visions?" she asked, looking me over.

"Cleo I'm fine, really," I insisted, stepping away. "It's been going on in bits and pieces ever since I was dead. I guess it'll all come back eventually."

"Yes," Cleo nodded, still frowning. "Just be careful."

"Why?" I asked. "I thought you were trying to help me remember."

"I know you want to remember your life," she said. "But just know it might not be what you've imagined."

By the time we got to the hospital the afternoon was flirting with evening. Though many others would be heading home around this time the building wasn't near closing time yet. The sky would tell you that it was around dinner, but the city was only just beginning to awaken. Traffic had picked up on our way here, although Cleo had promoted walking.

"DG, we might have to think this one through a bit more," Cleo advised as we walked the pathway to the hospital. "I can't move around as freely as you can."

"You're right," I realized, stopping to look up at the hospital. "We might have to find another way for you. We can wait until night."

"Oh no," Cleo insisted, shaking her head. "I don't want to break the law. I know this is important for you DG, so it's all right. It would be better that we go now."

Traffic was just starting to pick up as evening drew nearer. We were at the hospital doors now, and though there were few people around I wanted to watch out for Cleo.

"If you say so," I decided, waiting for her to open the door. I was glad I had actual access to all doors this time around. But I still missed the feeling of doing so myself. I hoped there were other ghosts that came about in the daytime, for a place closer to death than anywhere else in the city.

"And this girl, she's on the third floor in the pre-op room right?" Cleo alleged as she got the door.

I looked at her. "How'd you know?"

She smiled at me.

"Oh."

"The only question is," she went on while walked into the main lobby, "how do we get there?"

I didn't reply, trying to think it through in my head. Maybe I shouldn't have taken Cleo with me.

"I could pretend to be a visitor," she suggested, looking at me.

Just then, I noticed something out of the corner of my eye. "Come over here," I said suddenly, motioning for her to follow. We went around some chairs and I plopped myself in a seat behind some plants, which was mostly hiding my position. Cleo followed, a bit confused.

"DG, are you hiding?" she objected, her voice dropping to a whisper out of habit. "What's wrong?"

"Sit next to me," I replied, patting the seat next to me. She did, I double checking the lobby area.

"DG no one can see you," Cleo insisted, leaning forward to try and see what I was seeing. "What are you doing?"

It was them, Sarah and Rico. They were in the hospital lobby, looking around as they headed toward the exit. I knew they were important, but the third floor pre-op room would have to come first.

I didn't know what came over me. It was like I saw them and just had to hide; I'm not exactly sure why. What were they doing here? If they had broken into the hospital before, why would they come again in broad daylight?

And why did it seem like they were looking at me?

~

"I can help you get to the room but I can't stay long," Cleo explained as we climbed up the stairs. Once more Cleo insisted the journey be on foot, since she claimed that technology like an elevator interfered with her abilities. I didn't feel like arguing so I agreed.

"I know, I guess it's better if I see her alone," I decided, not too far behind. "Besides, she's kind of crazy. I don't want you to get hurt."

"I've handled crazy ghosts before," Cleo admitted, though I hardly believed her. "I had to chase an evil spirit out of my uncle's haunted cabin before."

I'm sure you did, I thought.

We got to the pre-op room. The sight of the hospital beds made my insides curdle. Yet this time I wasn't as afraid of the hospital. It was a lot less creepy-looking in the daylight, and the bustle of doctors and guests made it a lot less eerie.

"How long do you think you can stay up here?" I asked Cleo.

"Until someone catches me," she smiled.

I smiled back. "I thought you didn't want to break the law."

She shrugged. "They never said anything about visitors."

We came around the corner, almost to the point of Darla territory. I can't say I wasn't nervous, but I was doing my best not to show it.

"*You* again."

The voice sounded from the same area as before, the corner of one of the curtained off rooms. I jerked my head around, Cleo doing the same.

"I knew yous would come back."

"Darla?" Cleo asked in a hushed voice.

I nodded. "Darla."

"Ma'am, can I help you?" one of the nurses asked, glancing over at Cleo.

"Sickly, so sickly," Darla moaned. Her crouched shape began to crawl up from her dark corner. "So sickly since you tooks it."

"I'm just looking for a friend," Cleo replied to the nurse. "A— Henry Williams?"

The nurse frowned. "There is no Henry Williams up here. Only registered guests are allowed."

"Hurts, hurts, hurts, *hurts!*"

"I think she's onto you, Cleo," I noted.

Cleo turned to me. "Will you be all right?"

"Ma'am, I'm asking you to leave," the nurse said, giving her an impatient look. "I can call security."

"No, that'll be fine," Cleo insisted. "I'll go now."

She quickly turned and left, leaving me alone with the creature.

"Not so safes *now* that's yous on your own!" a voice barked from behind.

I whirled around. Darla suddenly crouched near my ankles. She was on all fours like some animal, snarling at me with a similar expression. In broad daylight, I got my first clear look at this spirit for the first time. She looked less intimidating in the daylight. Her hair used to be in curls, I think. Soft, tight curls had grown over a lifetime to splatter all over her face. They almost consumed it, her angry blue eyes poking through the mess.

"I's waits for you," she announced, pacing around my feet. "I's waits for the day I see the *murderer.*"

Again I was startled by how young this spirit was. Whatever had happened to her, she certainly didn't act like a child now.

"I need to talk to you," I explained. "Not fight, not hurt you. I just wanna talk."

"Talk he says," she repeated, stopping to pace in the opposite direction. "Yous thinks you can trick me twice?!"

"I'm not tricking," I insisted, holding up my arms. "Just talk, I swear. Why else would I come back?"

"Yous wants what yous took so yous comes back to take it again," Darla mumbled, snarling at me. Her words were almost too fast to be audible.

"And what did I take?" I asked, leaning down to get closer to her. "Tell me again."

"Blood! Blood! Yous takes my blood!" she shrieked, her hands grabbing my knees and her angry words in my face. "Yous takes blood yous murderer! Yous hateful, yous evil."

I held my ground, my voice rising. "How did I do it?"

"It's the knife," Darla proclaimed, jumping back with a wide-eyed expression. Her voice suddenly went into a soft, almost whisper-like tone. "The knife that touches the dead."

I leaned forward. "It happened when you were dead?"

"Good girl, I was," Darla insisted, nodding her head vigorously. "Good girl I was. I never hurts the people. I wants rest, rests in corner. I's happy there, I's peaceful."

Like any other territory ghost. "Then what happened?"

"Theys comes in the night," Darla went on in a dark, husky voice. She began to pace back and forth in front of me. "Theys come with the knife."

A knife that touches the dead. I was murdered with a knife, stabbed through the heart. Was it a coincidence? Could it be?

"And what did they do?" I asked again, keeping her talking. "What did they do with the knife?"

"Theys takes me to theirs lair." With each word a dark light seemed to grow in her eyes. "They keeps me in their lair. Darla can't get out. She tries and tries. They don't let Darla escape. They takes the knife, they takes it to Darla and—" she paused suddenly, as if something dawned on her. The dark expression faded into a wide-eyed confused one, her mouth slowly dropping open.

I moved forward. "Darla? Who did it?"

"Blood!" she shouted, hopping up and down, "blood blood blood blood blood. *Yous* dids it! Yous tooks it! Evil—horrible! Yous tooks it! Get *out.*"

She screamed, clutching her head with her hands and charging in my direction. I stumbled back, my deja vu telling me to get the heck out. I ran, squeezing past an open door. Before I knew it I was down the hall, throwing myself against the wall.

I could hear Darla's screams. I cringed, hearing her shriek while things in the room seemed to shake. Even the people seemed to look up from their work to notice. I waited against the wall and stared down the hallway, but she didn't come out. Thankful for the territorial boundary I had crossed, I made my way downstairs. Cleo and I had some more work to do.

Chapter 27

I found Cleo in the waiting room, sitting patiently in one of the chairs with a small book in her hands.

She caught my eye, seeing me on my way to her. "You look like you had an interesting discussion."

"Cleo, oh my gosh," I said, still catching up on my energy. "She's crazy. Absolutely crazy."

"But did you find out anything?" she asked, getting to her feet.

I nodded. "It's hard to believe all of it, but I did."

We were on our way back to Cleo's house. I tried to explain the best I could what had happened with Darla. I also told her about John West, the story Clyde told me.

"She said a knife that could touch the dead?" Cleo repeated, frowning. "I never heard of such a thing."

"Yeah, it sounds weird," I replied, hands in my pockets. "Do you think she's lying?"

"No, anyone in that state of mind doesn't think about lying much," Cleo thought out loud, looking at the sky. "Didn't you say a knife is what killed you?"

"Yeah but," I looked at her, "it can't be the same one, can it?"

"I'm not sure," Cleo looked up at the sky. "I wish I knew."

"But can't you figure it out? Being psychic and all?" I asked.

"I don't get to pick what I know," she explained. "Sometimes I have to figure out everything like anybody else. She was looking back at me. "You don't get to choose your powers. Only what you do with them."

"True," I nodded. "But what about the knife?"

"It sounds like the same person that hurt that poor girl is the same one that hurt you," Cleo figured. "Did she give any hints as to who it was?"

"She says I did it," I frowned, rethinking it. "But I couldn't have done it. Besides, the story about John West and Darla's tale are too similar."

"Of course," Cleo nodded. "Your death and Darla's experience were caused by the same person, and you didn't kill yourself. It does seem likely that this John West person is the culprit."

That still left a lot of things unanswered. "Then how could he kill me, especially if he's dead?"

"That's also true," she considered. "A lot of this doesn't make any sense."

Said the girl in the goat bandana. I kept my mouth shut.

"Why would he choose that poor little girl though?" Cleo asked, changing the subject. "She wasn't hurting anybody."

"Right," I replied. "Territorial ghosts keep to themselves, so she couldn't have been harming anybody. It does make her an easy target though."

In the distance, I could hear hushed whispers making their way down the street.

"Cleo," I said, stopping. "Wait up a sec. Listen."

She did, tilting her head to the side. "I hear talking. There's nothing wrong with that."

"No, no, no," I said, more to myself than her. "It's more than that. It's those people, the ones from before."

"Sarah and Rico?" Cleo asked. "They are on your mind a lot."

"Shh, they'll hear you!" I hushed, pulling into an alley. "Come in here."

"DG," Cleo insisted, "you can't hide from these things."

"Please," I begged, "just do it."

Cleo hesitated.

Two figures turned the corner, and Cleo obliged to step behind the building next to me. They had left the hospital when we came in, so they must have been wandering around town for hours or something. What were the up to?

"He's not there, and we're not any closer to the Reaper," the male voice, Rico, insisted.

"Not so loud." This voice was female. It was the girl, Sarah. They were coming along the sidewalk, now into our line of vision. They were passing, passing, almost passed.

"Don't move," I told Cleo, my voice falling to a whisper. I wasn't exactly aware why I was whispering, but it felt like the right thing to do. The way they had looked at me earlier, almost like as if they could see me.

One of the figures stopped.

"Sarah?"

It was Rico's voice. He turned to look at the girl, confused.

"Move," I told Cleo, my voice still low, "to the other side."

Cleo looked at me, like she wanted to protest but didn't want the figures to notice her.

"Please," I begged. I couldn't go talk to them, or follow them or whatever. Cleo was right here, and they could definitely see her. I couldn't just leave her.

She finally gave in, sliding along the wall to the other side of the alley. I led the way, making sure my footsteps remained quiet.

"Hey, you're ok right?" Rico smirked, as the two of them started heading down the alley. They had picked their conversation back up, but I didn't really take the time to pay attention. I had to get Cleo hidden, get out of here, think of something.

"Are you sure this is a good idea?" Cleo asked in the barest whisper.

I ushered her behind the corner, "Go, go, go, go!"

Cleo looked at me. "But why?"

"Shh," I replied in a hushed whisper. They heard me, I knew they heard me. But how was that even possible? I've followed them before, and they were oblivious before. What made things different now?

"Did you hear that, Rico?"

Sarah. The word came to my mind before I even realized it. That was Sarah, the girl from before, and the girl standing a few feet away. If I needed to talk to them, then why was I running away?

"No. What was it?"

Rico. The name brought a stir of something in my mind, the ghost of a forgotten memory. It was a fondness, and I knew then that he and I had been close. But why didn't I feel anything about Sarah?

"It almost sounded like—"

Cleo looked at me, a silent question of, *"What do we do?"* I waited.

"Like—"

I kept perfectly still, a dead man frozen in time. She had heard me, and she knew I was close. I closed my eyes, letting my sense of sound take over.

"Never mind."

She was disappointed. I had disappointed her. All this time spent searching and wondering, and I wasn't going to take the chance. That was cowardly of me. Seeing them in person suddenly made me chicken out, and now I was hiding behind a wall, running from my past. I needed to see them. They were the only connection to my life.

I turned to Cleo, holding up a hand in the universal 'wait' sign. I didn't have any breath to breathe in nervously, but I did have fists to clench. Preparing myself for whatever was about to happen, I stepped forward into the light.

I could see the two of them clearly now. Sarah was standing in the middle of the alley. Rico was at her side with a hand on her shoulder. He was giving her a sad look, but their eyes only saw each other. Not me.

I waited. Seconds went by, but the two figures remained the same. Was this it? Could they not see me? Had I really done all this for nothing?

"Lucas?"

I turned. Sarah was staring at me, her eyes not looking at the wall or the street, but at *me*. Stunned, I stared back, not able to say a word.

She left the arm of the boy. As if in slow motion, she broke away and ran toward me, bounding across the few feet between us. Before I knew what was happening she tackled me, her hug something both unexpected and surprisingly good.

She was hugging me. I could *feel* her touching me.

"Lucas!"

Chapter 28

I was forced to stumble back, but I was able to remain standing on my two feet. I didn't hug her back, but I certainly didn't push her away.

Lucas, is that what she called me? Is that who I was, the name I had had since birth?

"Where have you been?" she asked, breaking the hug to step back. "We looked everywhere. I waited for you!" She was happy to see me, but her tone was changing. There was something sadder growing in her eyes, something angry. "Why didn't you come? Why did you leave?"

I didn't know what to say. I didn't know who I was, much less where I was supposed to go. Something that struck me as odd was these people didn't react too much to the fact I was dead. They must have known; it had been a while. Apparently that wasn't a good enough excuse.

"I—"

"Long time, no see mate," Rico stepped up behind Sarah, smiling. "Well, still no see for me I guess. We were starting to think you'd gone on."

I didn't get it. He was smiling in my general direction, but he was facing a bit too much to the left. It took me a few seconds, but I realized Rico didn't have 'the sight.' He couldn't see me. But he still acted as if somehow he knew I was there.

"Well," I smiled back, not knowing what to say. "I didn't."

I knew these two. I was supposed to know these two. I had thought meeting them would bring back memories, that it would give me a path to remembering. But it didn't.

Sarah continued looking at me. She already knew something was wrong. "You were here this whole time. Why didn't you come find us Lucas?"

I looked from one expecting face to the other, more lost than ever. How could I explain that I just forgot? *I* don't even understand it. With one last failed attempt to recall either of these people, I opened my mouth.

"I—I'm sorry. I couldn't find you. I didn't know how."

The two faces in front of me were confused. I looked at Sarah, the girl who had been so thrilled to see me again. Her eyes searched me for some kind of answer I didn't have. She knew me well enough to know I was speaking the truth. That much I could pick up. But she didn't understand why, or how. I could practically see the thoughts forming in her eyes.

Then there was Rico, who didn't express much through his hungry, intense stare. I could see his confusion, but he was more reserved in his actions. He looked as if he were listening intently for me to say something.

"What do you mean Lucas?" Sarah asked, stepping back. "Did something— has something come up?"

"I— no. Well—"

"Don't worry DG, it's not your fault," a voice sided with me. Cleo stepped out from behind the corner. To tell you the truth I had almost forgotten she was there. She had been listening the whole time, her brown eyes greeting each face as she placidly made her way toward us.

"Who is that?" Sarah asked, half to me and half to herself. "Are you dead?"

"I'm alive, don't worry," Cleo smiled. "I'm Cleopatra. Your friend can't remember much, I'm afraid. He lost his memory."

Sarah and Rico looked at each other. Things were getting more and more complicated, for all of us.

"Who's DG? What do you mean?" Sarah asked, not getting it. She didn't want to get it. She looked at me. "Is this true?"

She wasn't mad, I could tell she wasn't. Rico was all right too. It wasn't that, it was disappointment.

"Yes," I admitted, and I could feel her face drop. "I lost my memory. I couldn't come find you because I didn't know about you."

"But you're here now," she pointed out, still confused. "How did you come back if you didn't know?"

I looked from one face to the other. "I found your photos after some research," I shifted to the other foot, unsure. "And I overheard you say something about the Reaper."

"The Reaper," Rico repeated, his already intense eyes lighting up. "Did you learn anything about him?"

"No, I thought you knew more," I replied. So Rico could hear me. I was relieved they were familiar with the term, but also worried. They expected me to know something they didn't, and I was even more clueless than them.

"That's the thing Lucas," Sarah said, turning to me. "There's a lot more to this than what you'd think."

I frowned. "What do you mean?"

"That all depends on what you remember," Rico joined in, stepping next to Sarah. "Can you recap?"

I did the best I could. I explained most of what I've learned from the knife to the book hidden in the library. I left out the parts about Rowley and Clyde – it was too much to explain in one day. For now, I kept it to the facts, and hopefully I'd have time to tell the rest later.

"But you don't know who the Reaper is?" Sarah asked, leaning forward.

I searched my memory. I searched it again. It seemed like Sarah knew what I was talking about. Something in her voice told me I was supposed to know who the Reaper was.

But that was before I lost it all, before I couldn't remember. Looking into her eyes, I made my best guess.

"John West?"

Rico coughed suddenly, as if he swallowed something wrong. Sarah gasped, going wide eyed at my own words.

"John West," Sarah began, shocked. It was the first time her voice actually made me jump. "Is that some kind of joke?"

"No," I said matter-of-factly, "I wouldn't joke about something like this. Why, what's wrong with John West?"

"Who told you that?" Sarah pressed, suddenly angry and curious and frightened. "Who said that about your father?"

Chapter 29

Transaction

Rowley remained still as he hung in the air, waiting. The door closed. Alder locked it.

"What's up boss?" Rowley asked, a hint of worry in his tone.

Clyde returned to his seat, his hands neatly folded on the desk top. He had asked to see his friend Rowley and he came, just as he expected. It was a private audience, of course. Things were always cleaner that way. If this transaction went according to plan, as Clyde Harrison's deals usually did, he and Alder were going to make quite a significant profit.

"So Rowley," he started off, looking up at the floating figure. "How's William doing?"

Rowley paused, his expression hardening. "He's fine."

"Fine? Just fine?" Clyde asked, surprised as he reached into his desk drawer. "I didn't expect that of you. Surely you've seen him since your friend DG arrived. He had a game tonight, didn't he? You haven't introduced DG?"

Rowley remained still.

"No."

"No? No matter, it will come in time, yes?" he smiled, closing the drawer. He had it sitting in the second drawer on the left, Rowley knew it. "He'll be going to college soon, right?"

"Yeah, next year."

"They grow up so fast," Clyde said to himself, and Rowley could feel the old griping regret creep up. "Tuitions are expensive these days. I wonder how he'll pull it off."

"You know how." Rowley's gaze had shifted to floor, but he knew. He knew what Clyde wanted, and he knew what would happen.

"I had another customer this morning, did you notice him?" Clyde went on, his tone conversational.

Rowley nodded, he saw the customer, "Yeah." He didn't realize until now what the man had wanted to purchase.

"Now, I'm just the middle man in these kinds of things. But I think I've worked out a deal for you two, haven't I?"

"I guess so." Rowley remained quieter than usual, the realization sinking in. He hadn't thought about this in years. He didn't think the time would come up again, not so soon. But he knew there was always a chance.

"I need another payment, Rowley."

Rowley nodded, knowing there was no point in arguing. It had been so long since the last time. Rowley had hoped—

convinced himself he would no longer have to give payments. He had gone through too much the last time. He swore he wouldn't do it again. But Will was worth sacrificing for.

"I promise," Clyde started, rising from his seat, clasping it in his hand, "this one will be quick."

"I know," Rowley nodded, drifting closer to the businessman. But he stopped a few feet away, suddenly getting cold feet. "And you promise to pay for it?"

"Tuition, books, room and board, the works," Clyde agreed. "No loopholes, no suspicions, no traces, just the money. Your family will never know."

"All right," Rowley agreed, crossing the final distance.

Clyde hesitated. "Did it hurt the last time?" He was curious. Of course there was pain, there always was. Perhaps, Clyde hoped, it wasn't as strong. Rowley had given payments before, perhaps he was accustomed to it.

"Not as much," Rowley answered honestly. He knew what to expect now. Clyde positioned the weapon, ready to strike when Rowley pulled away. "What about DG?"

"I'm sure your friend will be able to manage on his own while you're— resting," Clyde smiled encouragingly. "You've been good to him."

"Yeah," Rowley smiled, more to himself than Clyde. "I guess I have." He moved closer to Clyde.

"You've always been a good sport."

Rowley closed his eyes. He had trouble finding his voice. "I know."

And with that, Clyde sunk the dagger into Rowley's soul.

Chapter 30

Lucas

"My father?"

My mouth fell open, I couldn't help it. Clyde had said John West had been dead, long dead. I assumed he meant years, decades even. I didn't expect him to be alive within my lifetime.

"John and Madeline West," Sarah repeated, looking at me earnestly. "Don't you know those names?"

I shook my head. Of course I knew about John West, but the name didn't strike me as familiar. His dark hair and eyes that I had seen in the photograph in Clyde's album did slightly resemble my own, but I had never given much thought to that. John West was a killer.

"You really don't remember?"

I shook my head again.

"Well this is pretty messed up," Rico decided, pacing as he scratched his head. "Who told you about John West?"

We continued our walk, while I did my best to recap my afterlife's story, Clyde and Rowley included. The walk looked silent to the Chicago dwellers, but Sarah and Rico were listening intently. They didn't interrupt, even when I mentioned seeing them at the hospital. Near the end of my tale, we ended up in the park, the sun near setting.

"You can see why we were so confused," Cleo added when I was finished. "We honestly didn't know."

"What were you guys doing all this time?" I asked them.

"Trying to find a way to stop the Reaper," Rico replied. "And, you know, mourning our dead best friend."

"We thought you'd come back, even just for a few hours to say goodbye," Sarah added. "We were worried about you."

I looked out at the soon-to-be night sky, my mind trying to unravel what was going on around me. Rico and Sarah were finally here, at my side. To them, it was three friends reunited. To me, it was just another unfilled memory. How could I explain that to them?

"It's getting a little late to continue with the story sharing," Cleo noted, looking at the sky. "My parents will probably want me home soon. It's vegan night."

"For those of us that eat, anyway," Rico smirked, and I knew he was talking about me.

"I'm still coming with you," I insisted, brushing Rico's remark aside, "or with one of you. Where are you going?"

"Beats me," Rico shrugged. He looked at Sarah, "Your place?"

"Oh no." She shook her head. "I am not doing ghost stuff at my house. My parents will freak out. Yours?"

"Sure," he shrugged again. "I think there's food there."

"I'm afraid I won't be able to join you," Cleo chimed in. "I have to meet with my three a.m. appointment on the lost souls of the Civil War."

"That's fine," Rico replied, as if that was like any other normal excuse. "I guess we'll have another sleepover at my place then."

~

The apartment where Rico lived wasn't that big, but it was big enough for us. His parents had gone out of town for the weekend, so it was just the three of us tonight. On entering the premises I expected to be flooded with memories. Instead I got something different. As I stepped through the door into the kitchen/dining room/living room area all within one hundred feet of each other, I didn't get a memory. I got of feeling. It was a feeling of relief and safety, that everything was at ease. It felt familiar, like a second home.

"So you've met Darla and Lyly," Rico was saying, commenting on my story of the library. "That makes things easier."

"Yeah," I smiled. "Is his name really Lyly Berry?"

"Nah, it's a nickname," Rico shrugged. He was slightly facing the wrong way, but I could work with that.

"How do you know them? Actually, how do you know anything about this?"

"Vocals man," Rico informed while pointing to his ear. "That's all I get."

"We stick together, the ones with the gift," Sarah explained. "It makes the whole psychic thing feel more normal."

"So you can see me?" I clarified.

"You're a bit fuzzy, but yeah," she agreed. "I wasn't born with the gift, so it's hard to see sometimes."

I frowned. "How'd you get your gift then?" I was fine with psychics, but I wasn't ready to handle sorcery being real too.

"I was really young," she began. "My family was at a funeral for one of our neighbors. That was the first ghost I ever saw." The memory seemed to make her tense. She crossed her arms and continued. "I tried to leave the building but my parents wouldn't let me. I had to stand there while that thing stood over its body."

"That's awful." I found myself crossing my arms as well. When I saw ghosts for the first time I had acted like a total pansy. Sarah didn't get that luxury. On the flip side, my own experience with my body had been similarly tragic. But I couldn't imagine coming to my own funeral.

"The next day it seemed to take root in its family's house," she recalled. "It followed my neighbors. It followed them everywhere. And when it figured out I had the sight, it followed me too." She shook her head. "As a kid I never thought of it as a ghost. I thought it was a monster or the Boogey Man."

I watched Sarah talk. It looked like a part of her was still nervous when mentioning this ghost, despite the fact she was speaking to one. "So what did you do?"

"I moved," she answered. "Or rather, my parents did. My dad got a new job, and I wasn't fairing so well in our current living condition."

She looked at me, waiting for a reaction. Rico just listened the whole time, not really paying attention to the story he's probably heard before.

"That is a weird way to get the sight," I finally agreed. "Why then?"

"I don't know," she shrugged. "After we moved I rarely saw any other ghosts. It only acted up again when I met you guys in high school."

"That I knew about," I reminded them. "And then we all met up and got involved with the Reaper?"

"What you were told was sort of true. Your father died when you were very young," Sarah explained. "Only it was the Reaper that tried to consume a spirit, and he died trying to stop him. When the police found him, it looked like a suicide. But you would never believe that he took his own life."

"Pretty rough for a little kid," Rico commented.

"Then when you found one of your dad's old journals, you started looking into it a lot more." I nodded, feeling rather disconnected to my own past. "In all our research we never found a name, just the Reaper story."

"Sure, 'research.' More like obsession," Rico mumbled.

"Then we all started doing research together, like that book you found in the library. We started looking into random murders and unexplained deaths in the city. Only again, it was hard to trace it back to one person."

"Plus you needed evidence," I pointed out.

"Well, we're still working on that," Sarah shrugged, "including some interviews with ghosts."

I stopped her. "I had the gift?"

"You inherited it through your father," Sarah said. "Like I said, mine's not that good. It works better when I'm around others who can see. We're not really sure why it happens, but," she shrugged, smiling at me, "it did." I nodded. That explained why they hadn't found me earlier. I must have been too far away for her to pick up anything.

"Anyway, about the whole Reaper thing," Rico began again. "You tried doing something a bit more dangerous.

You said you started following suspects, spying and all that. I don't even know what you found out, but that's when you died."

I looked across the room, not that he could tell. "Oh."

"We don't have to think about it though," Sarah cut in, looking at me. "We're just glad to have you back."

Chapter 31

That night was the most normal night in my afterlife. The two of them ordered pizza. We sprawled out on an out-of-style shag carpet and watched unlimited movies on pay-per-view. The sky slowly faded to night. The rustle of cars and screech of the L train cars all seemed far away. We talked, but the conversation wasn't focused on the Reaper or the fact I was dead. They reminded on the crazy stunts we had done in the past, and how they had been. I talked too. The words felt right, as if I hadn't forgotten who these people were. It was good to be off of the streets. And for the first time, I felt like I belonged.

It took five minutes for Rico to pull out his guitar, and two hours before he'd put it away. His whole life was music, and he played about a hundred different instruments. The song I heard when I first met Cleo, he used to play it all the time. He also knew millions of others. It didn't take long for me to notice the constant air drumming, or tapping out measures on random surfaces. He had a great ear, whether for the dead or just a melody. He told me how we used to get ghosts to read notes we wrote in class out loud, so we could talk without passing them.

Then there was Sarah. She had met us early in high school, and hung around ever since. When she first got glimpses of ghost as a kid, she freaked out and thought she was going insane. She had been avoiding the dead ever since she got her gift. Then after meeting Rico and me, Sarah finally came to terms with it. We'd hung out together the past school year and had grown really close, all of us. She had me help her with her gift, and we had spent the majority of weekends together. There was something else about her too, but I couldn't put my finger on it.

"Hey," I said, sitting up. The three of us were on the floor, slouched against the foot rest on the couch facing the TV. "I didn't know you had a cat."

On the arm of the couch, an orange and black cat perched above our heads, its yellow eyes regarding us with displeasure. It yawned, displaying its fangs as a warning.

"Sweet," Rico replied, looking around the room. "Where is he?"

"That's Marvin," Sarah told me, craning her neck to see the feline. "He's hung around the apartment ever since Rico's family moved here."

I gave her a confused look.

Sarah re-phrased herself. "He's dead."

"Don't say that in front of him," Rico protested. "You'll hurt his feelings."

To my shock, the displeasured cat stretched from its perch, slowly coming down to us in long, lazy strides. To my amusement, it rubbed against me as it passed, its tail swishing across my nose. It made its way to Rico, where it rubbed its face against his shoulder and purred.

"I can hear him," Rico smiled, reaching over hesitantly with the other hand, "and feel him."

"You're getting better Rico," Sarah smiled. "He never comes over for anybody."

"That's 'cause he likes me best," Rico smirked, picking up the cat he couldn't see with ease, "isn't that right Marvin?"

"You're crazy," I decided, smiling.

"How's he doing today?" Rico asked, setting the feline on his lap as he began to stroke him. "What does he look like?"

"He's orange and black," I explained, staring at the house cat with intense eyes, "like patches. And he looks like an angry philosopher."

"That's a pretty good mood for Marvin," Sarah told me. "I think he missed you."

"Right," I sighed. A cat was the least of my worries.

The night drew on. Like most living people, Sarah and Rico needed sleep. Rico passed out somewhere in the middle of a sitcom. Sarah remained awake, only enough to watch the television with me. Marvin would come and go. Sometimes he would even come to let me pet him, and I was perfectly fine petting the dead cat.

"It's nice," Sarah said, breaking the hour long silence, "to be together again." Her hair was tossed over her shoulder, head propped up by an arm leaning lazily into the couch.

"Yeah," I sighed, "I miss remembering it."

"Do you really not remember?" she asked, turning to her side to look at me. "You don't remember anything?"

"Nothing I didn't already tell you," I replied. She really asked that a lot. It felt like she was waiting, waiting for something to come that I didn't know about.

"I figured." She sighed and looked back at the TV. "I wish you did though."

"You and me both," I shrugged, leaning back even more into the couch. "I keep trying to find memories, really I do. I've been trying to find something that'll help. Nothing ever does though."

She looked back at me. "Did this help?"

"In a way," I replied honestly. "It didn't remind me of anything, but it gave me a certain feeling of— something, I guess." I couldn't give a name to it.

"Of what?" Sarah asked, scouting closer.

I turned to look at her. "Home."

It was in that moment I realized how close Sarah was to me. Not just physically, where I could feel her breath on my face. But I felt her mentally. She had been sticking close to me. I could tell she'd wanted to badger me all night ever since we were reunited. But she was giving me my space. It was like she wanted to ask about something, but knew it was better to keep it to herself.

"We were dating," I said. It wasn't a question. It was a fact. I hadn't thought about it much, but from seeing the two of them hang out so much I had almost assumed that Rico and Sarah were somehow together. They'd been with each other this whole time. I had forgotten it was me she was looking for.

I wasn't worried about Rico though. There was another problem. I couldn't be with Sarah anymore. What's worse, the thought hadn't even crossed my mind. It was so much different being dead. I didn't notice people— women— the same way you'd think a guy normally should when he's alive. I hadn't thought about romance or love, or anything like that. I didn't have a body. I didn't have hormones.

"Do you remember it?" she asked, inching ever so slightly closer. "Or did you just figure it out?"

"I wish I could tell you I remember," I replied. Every word of it was true. I felt bad for leaving this girl— my girlfriend— alone in the world now that I had died. And what's worse, now that I'm actually here I didn't, *couldn't*, have the same feelings for her as she did for me. I wish I could tell her otherwise, but it wasn't true.

Sarah leaned back into the couch. "It's alright if you don't," she laughed, more to herself than at me. "I wouldn't expect you to, what with the memory loss and all."

She was lying, and she deserved better. I looked down, where her was almost on top of mine. It was at that moment it dawned on me. Sarah could touch spirits, like Cleo and Clyde could. Well, maybe not exactly like them. Her gift was stronger around other psychics. She had hugged me earlier, and she could touch me now.

I moved my fingers to intertwine with hers. "We can still feel each other."

"I know. It's always been stronger around others, but," she looked at me, "it's always been the strongest around you."

What would happen after I left? Would Sarah lose her gift?

"I'm sorry," I frowned, "about all this."

"It's not your fault," she sighed, looking away. "You're dead. You'll be gone in a few weeks."

"Hey," I cut in, looking her in the eye. "Don't worry about that now."

She managed a sliver of a smile. "I know."

"It's not on purpose," I told her, a hint of sadness in my voice. "I didn't mean for this to happen. I'm sorry I left you."

"It's not your fault," she told me again, reaching over to touch me. "It isn't."

"Still," I insisted, even though it wasn't romantic thing to say, "I'm dead."

"But you're here now," she smiled, "and that's what's important."

Then it came out, not bound by a body or something in the brain. It wasn't a memory, or the feeling of a memory. It was a part of me. "I love you."

She smiled, wiping something from her eyes. "I love you too."

She could touch me, our fingers slowly wrapping around each other. Maybe, just maybe—

I reached out, hesitantly, and brushed a hair on her face. To my own surprise, the hair moved, and my fingers guided the strand toward the rest of her soft hair, gazing some skin as it past. She was soft, warm— alive. I wasn't even there, technically, yet she was standing there as a breathing, living creature.

I leaned forward, unsure of myself as ever. Whatever guided me, whatever feelings that possessed me, were strong ones. I kissed her forehead, slow and surely as the memories spread through my brain and down my neck. Her whole body gave off heat, a moving creature against the still chilliness of my own soul. Below me I felt Sarah close her eyes, the silence around us filling in what words could never fully say. Words weren't needed.

I could never be with the living. They moved me and shoved me around without feeling it. Even with psychics in the picture I could never truly move them back. The dead didn't belong here, not on this planet. We needed the closure only to move on to the next step of existence. Sarah and I both knew this relationship could never be what it had been. It couldn't last beyond this night.

I couldn't make up for my lack of body. I couldn't come back to life and promise both of us everything would be ok. But we could touch, and that was enough.

Chapter 32

It was a few hours before Sarah fell asleep. We had a good talk. I know it was nothing like it should have been. It wasn't up to living standards I guess. We didn't focus on the problems going on around us. All that could wait until tomorrow. This was the first time we had been alone, and maybe the only chance we would have for a proper goodbye.

She fell asleep next to Rico, curled between the foot of the couch and the floor. I had a feeling that wasn't new for any of us. I still felt bad and wanted to help. I picked up her hand, making her fingers curl around a blanket hanging over the couch. Using her hand, I pulled it over the two of them. Maybe they'd be a bit more comfortable that way.

Marvin sensed the two living creatures were asleep, and prowled over to me for mandatory stroking. I obliged, leaning back on the couch to face the still glowing TV. Knowing it was to no use to me I picked up Sarah's hand again and slapped it on the remote, shutting off the muted image. With a single click, the room seemed to be even quieter than before. Even Marvin was silent, his golden eyes half closed in contentment.

The living were asleep, and I was alone again.

Chapter 33

I was hoping my friends weren't the kind of teenagers to sleep in. Thankfully they were up by nine. They took a while to be ready, having to eat and all. We were sitting at Rico's kitchen table, the two of them eating the leftovers of several combined cereal boxes while I sat in the chair and waited. I hadn't thought about eating much. I was never hungry, and I never craved food. But being the only one abstaining made me miss the experience.

"Dude, you gotta say something," Rico said, putting down his bowl. "I can't even tell if you're here anymore."

"Hm? I'm here," I announced, sitting up a bit.

"What do you dead people do all night?" Rico asked, curiously looking up into a space I wasn't sitting.

"Oh," I poked his hand and he jerked around to a more accurate area at my voice. "That's the weird thing about ghosts. They don't do much."

"It seems boring," Rico frowned, getting up with his bowl hanging in one hand, "hanging around for centuries. I don't see how you do it."

"I wasn't really planning on it," I shrugged, before realizing he couldn't really see that. "I mean, I wasn't planning on staying at all really. Before, I mean."

Rico frowned, putting his dishes in the sink.

"Has that changed at all since you found us?" Sarah asked, looking at me.

I paused. For some reason, Alder came to my mind. He was obviously an older ghost, but he stuck around to be with Clyde. It seemed like an unworthy cause, following your friends around like a shadow. I loved my friends, and I wanted to find all my memories for sure. But was it worth living as one of the dead?

I frowned. "I don't know."

~

We were finishing up breakfast, the TV filling the background with mindless jibber jabber under our own conversation. Rico and Sarah had just plopped themselves on the couch when the phone rang.

"Got it," Rico announced, leaning forward from his seat. He made the effort to flop his hand on top of his phone, barely a few feet from him. By luck, he managed to hit the speaker button.

"Is this Rico's phone?" A familiar voice asked, skipping introductions.

I leaned forward. "Cleo?"

"Oh good, you are still with them," Cleo replied. She sounded relieved and tired, like she was out of breath.

"Hey. How did you get this number?" Sarah asked, confused.

"I had a feeling," Cleo explained simply, "a strong one. Though I admit it wasn't my first guess."

"We can talk about that later," I cut in. I didn't want to think about Cleo calling strangers. "What happened?"

"I think something happened to Rowley."

"Rowley?' Rico repeated, forgetting the name for a second.

"What makes you think that?" I asked, suddenly concerned.

"I had a dream— it was really awful, DG," Cleo told me. "Or, I'm sorry, do you want to be called Lucas now?"

"Never mind," I protested. "What happened to Rowley?"

"I'm not quite sure," Cleo replied, a worried tone in her voice. "That's what I'm afraid of. Do you think you can contact him?"

"I— I don't know," I replied honestly. "I wasn't sure where he went yesterday. I could ask Clyde maybe?"

"No!" Cleo broke in, cutting me off with a sharp tone that wasn't like her. "Don't do that. I'm not sure what, but there's something dangerous in that man's office."

"Did Clyde do something to Rowley?" I asked alarmed.

"I don't know," Cleo replied sympathetically. "But don't go there. It's dangerous."

"Then where is Rowley?" I asked again.

"Oh no," Sarah said, her eyes downcast. She slowly looked up at us, a worried expression in her eyes. "I think I know."

~

"And how do you know where Rowley lives?" I asked, running next to Sarah. The three of us were back out in the city, the morning heat not yet settled in. We darted across the street and slowed to a walk, where Rico was able to catch up.

"I don't know why I didn't see it before," Sarah said to herself, shaking her head.

"Ok, what is all this about?" Rico asked, unknowingly coming between us.

She looked at him. "Will Hart."

I turned to her. "What did you say?"

"Will Hart," Rico frowned. "What does that guy have to do with anything?"

"Will," I repeated, nodding. "Rowley knows a guy named Will. He's his brother." I frowned. "Why is he important?"

"Yes, they were brothers," Sarah nodded. Her face was scrunched in concentration, collecting her memories while trying to plan our path. "I can't believe I forgot his name!"

"You forgot Will's name?" Rico questioned.

"You knew Rowley?"

"No," Sarah said, waving her hands in front of her face. "I mean, yes. Kind of."

"Ok, can you explain this more clearly?" I sighed.

"The Harts were old neighbors of mine," Sarah explained, quickening her pace. "We were friends for a little while before I moved. Sometimes I still see them around after school."

I remembered that school Rowley and I had found that picture. He knew his way around, even though he had never gone to high school.

"We don't talk that much now," Sarah continued. "And I think you know why."

"What does Will have to do with this?" I pressed.

"It's how I got my sight," Sarah sighed, stopping in front of an apartment complex. I stopped too. I remembered the story she told me yesterday, the one about the ghost in her neighbor's house.

I paused to think for a second. "So mean Rowley—?"

"Yes," Sarah admitted. "But we don't have time for explanations. He should be in there, you can ask him yourself."

Chapter 34

I stared at her like she was crazy.

"We can't go in without looking like trespassers," she explained. Ah yes, it was illegal to break into an apartment. Not everyone was as carefree as Cleo. "Not in broad daylight. You have to go in on your own."

"We'll wait for you out here, don't worry." Rico smiled in the wrong direction.

Sarah turned his head the right way. "He's in that window, in 432."

I wasn't too keen on doing this. Even with the whole law thing aside, it felt like I was trespassing on Rowley's life. He was so private about the whole thing I figured he wouldn't want me in there. Besides, what had happened to him?

I was hesitant, but eventually gave in. I allowed my girlfriend to convince me to climb through an open window. How'd I get to the fourth floor? The convenience of a fire escape. I'll admit it was a tight fit. But I've found my lack of body helps me crawl through any space a small child could get through. After tumbling onto the kitchen floor, I craned my neck to get a good look at the place.

"Rowley?"

He was hovering over an empty chair. Rowley hung in the air like a floating rag doll. His expression was solemn— no, blank. It was something I'd never seen on him before. His entire presence was complete with sunken, glazed eyes. It was the opposite of the happy-go-lucky kid I had met on the street.

"Rowley!" I said again, running over to him. This wasn't right. Something was definitely wrong. But at least I had found him. "Hey, Rowley, where have you been?"

Rowley said nothing, his glazed eyes seeing nothing but the family that lived in the house. He gave no recognition that I was even there.

"Rowley? Hey, Rowley?" I asked again, reaching up to shaking his shoulder a bit. He swayed back and forth, but the ghost said nothing. "Hey!"

"What time do you get out of practice today?" the woman, the mother, asked the teenage boy at the table.

"I think two, that's nothing," the boy answered between mouthfuls of cereal. "Besides, we creamed them last night."

"How was the game last night?" the father asked, looking up and taking interest.

"Good," the boy replied.

"Rowley, what are you doing here?" I asked, turning back to him. He said nothing. The image was starting to freak me out. Here, hanging in this room, Rowley, the one guy who looked so much more alive than anyone I'd seen in the city, looked so dead.

"You don't have to do this on your own," the father said, turning to the table. "We can always pitch in if you need it."

"No," the son said. "If I win this game, I get the scholarship. I don't want you guys to worry."

The father smiled. "That's my boy."

This didn't make sense. Sarah said this was Rowley's family. But I'd seen his brother. Will Hart was like, five. This wasn't the right family, this wasn't the right house.

Rowley mumbled something.

I turned to him. "What?"

But he wasn't responding to me, almost like I wasn't there. Slowly, I turned back to the table. An only child and a couple sat at a table set for four. The father said something and he laughed, his green eyes lighting up in a way I had seen before. The one empty chair, the only empty chair, was the exact same one Rowley hovered over. He resigned himself to watching, a sense of longing in his sad green eyes. But it couldn't be.

"Rowley," I started slowly, walking toward the boy. "Is this your family?"

"Don't touch him!"

Rowley suddenly snapped back into reality, awake and angry, darting from his spot to put himself between me and his brother. "Don't you *ever* touch him."

"Rowley!" I stammered in shock, stepping back. It was the first thing that came out of my mouth. "Hey, I didn't know."

"Get out of my house," he snapped, his face twisted in a look of rage. "Get away from them. You can't have them!"

I frowned, confused and angry at the same time. "I'm not going to steal them."

"This is *my* house! *My* family. Get away from them!"

I glanced at the window I had come through. It was still there, ready for escape. But Rowley had cut me off from my exit, forcing me to stepping back. Even if I did charge past him, I was almost positive he would follow me.

"Rowley, I can't get out."

"He hates ghosts!" Rowley shouted, eyes boring into mine. "Twelve years, three months and five days, and he still hates ghosts. You'll scare them. *All* of them. *Get. Out!*"

He was pushing me back, closer and closer until I had backed up against a wall. To be honest as much as I was ready to sock him, I was terrified. This was Rowley, the guy who made jokes about pedestrians and laughed all the way through his afterlife. What had gotten into him?

"Rowley, snap out of it," I started, but he wasn't listening. He had backed away now, zooming back and forth in some odd way of pacing.

"What am I gonna do, DG?" he asked. He did a complete one eighty, sounding more terrified than furious. "I can't go. I can't leave them. Clyde's gonna help me, help them, he promised. I do what he tells me to. I don't wanna leave them."

"Rowley— it's— it's ok" I tried, watching him with concern. He kept going back and forth, as if he didn't know I was there. Twelve years, did he say, twelve years? This place was his home, his source of energy. He had stayed here, watching his family grow without him for twelve years.

"It's ok," he repeated, nodding, smiling to himself. "Clyde'll take care of it. Clyde said he knows what to do. He helps, he always helps."

I watched with growing fear. Rowley said he was in debt to Clyde, that Clyde had a lot of souls in debt. And with Clyde being the only effective communication with the living, I could see why.

"What happened?" I asked, hoping not to get screamed at again.

"It's done, it's done. I already paid for it. Clyde had me pay for it. It didn't hurt much. Not really. Not the fourth time."

"Paid for what? How?" I asked.

"I couldn't tell you before, DG," Rowley explained, still zooming back and forth. "I was going to let Clyde break the news to you. Break it slowly, you know? That's how he likes to do things. We couldn't let you find out before you were ready."

Rowley was keeping something from me? "Ready for what?"

"We can't tell you, DG," Rowley apologized, his face now downcast toward the floor. "We just— I can't."

There was something wrong with Rowley, but I couldn't tell what. None of this was like him. This emotional breakdown or whatever it was freaked me out.

Cleo was right, something was definitely up. And I knew the man who had the answers. It was time to visit Clyde.

Chapter 35

"Is everything all right?"

Cleo had made it to the house. I was about to ask how, but then I remembered the whole psychic thing. She was standing with Rico and Sarah, who had no doubt filled her in on the whole thing. Including the family part.

"Rowley's not coming out," I explained as I came down the fire escape. "It's pretty bad."

"Well we can't go in there," Sarah pointed out, gesturing toward the house. "How can we get him to come out?"

"He's the one that'll know what's going on," Cleo agreed.

"I'm not sure he does," I frowned, glancing back at the house. "He's too out of sorts. We can't talk to him."

"Why not?" Rico asked. "Just grab the dude and throw him out."

"He'll come around on his own," I told them. "He just needs—" I remembered what he told me earlier, "energy. He needs energy from his own home. Besides there's something else I gotta do."

"What?"

"DG," Cleo started, "I told you, you can't go to the office."

"Why not?" I protested. "I'm dead. Whatever he's got there can't be that bad. Isn't he the only one that knows what's going on right now? Rowley won't tell."

"Where's he going?" Sarah asked Cleo, still confused.

"He shouldn't go at all," Cleo replied, looking at me. "DG, please don't."

"Wait for Rowley to come out. I'll come back here when I'm done," I insisted.

I didn't wait for a response from anyone. I took off, darting down the street.

"Which way did he go?" Rico asked, looking around wildly. It didn't matter. I was gone.

~

Across the street. Up the stairs. Down the hall. It felt weird to make this journey on my own for the first time. I reached the door, stopping for my energy to recharge. The door to Clyde's office was flung open, but no one was there. I waited, looking down the hall. No one was coming either. Deciding he must have been out or in some kind of meeting, I walked in.

Even Alder was out. I never knew if he followed Clyde everywhere or waited here, but he was gone. No one was in the room. Should I wait for him to come back or go look for him? Unsure, I walked about the room.

The desk was empty, his chair off to the side like he had left in a hurry. On the desktop, the book with his clients was sitting on top of the work pile. Curious, I leaned forward, one hand on the desktop, reading what it said.

This page was different from the one Clyde had showed me. It didn't hold a client's information but past transaction's and work information.

George Long: applied 4/15/13.

Transaction: 2 million per 8oz.

Donor: Rowley Hart, 7/22/13

Notes: An approximate minus 60 on first use, stronger effects within the first few days.

I read the page again— and again. The date next to the donor part was yesterday, the day Rowley had left. How could Rowley have been a 'donor?' What could Rowley give when he didn't even own anything?

"He's using them! That's how he does it!"

The words echoed through my brain, the memory still unclear. He had done something to Rowley, right here in this office. The very same spot I was standing.

And he used him— used him for what?

It was then I remembered Darla's words on blood.

"Lucas!"

I knew the voice, but how did the voice know me?

"I'm so glad you made it. I was starting to second-guess myself."

I turned and saw Clyde standing in the doorway. His business smile couldn't have picked a better day to beam on his face. His grin held something sinister.

"You know, you really made me think through this one," he started, strolling over to me. I took a step back, trying to maintain a heated look on my face. "You almost had me. You *almost* had me." He chuckled, waving a finger. "I did every test I could think of and you *passed!* You have my congratulations."

"What tests?" I asked. He had lied to me my whole afterlife. Why should I believe anything he said now?

"Lucas," Clyde said, smiling at me, "the game is over. We can talk now, you and me. Man to ghost, am I right?"

He had me. He had caught me like a rat in a trap. Alder soon appeared by the doorway, blocking my only exit.

"I don't know what you're talking about," I replied, backing away. The desk was the only thing that stood between us. Alder could easily fix that.

"You're good at playing dumb," Clyde complimented. "I tried *everything*. I told you your father was a murderer. I told you I could help you. I shamed, killed, and fooled your past life in every way possible and you took every word without batting an eye. It was almost like you believed me. You have a gift Lucas. A gift!"

"You lied about my father?" I asked, trying to keep him talking. The door was out. I had to think of a different exit strategy.

"Of course I did," Clyde frowned, believing I was fully aware of this. "Switched the characters around a bit, right? You know the story."

It was official: John West was Innocent. My *father* was innocent. I kept talking.

"You killed my father," I growled.

"Yes," Clyde nodded, bowing at the compliment. "The poor little Lucas West. His mother died at childbirth and his father dead by the time the boy was age four. Such a tragic story, isn't it?"

He was baiting me, but it wasn't going to work. My eyebrow twitched, and as the words sunk in I realized this man had taken everything away from me. He took my family, my reputation, my life. But I wouldn't let him win. I had to keep it together.

"I wouldn't have intervened if you hadn't insisted on meddling. So much like your father," Clyde jeered.

I suddenly felt hot, angry. If I let him aggravate me too much, I lost. I couldn't do it. I had to stay calm.

"And now you have nothing left I can take from you. You're just a shadow, really. You don't have anything worth stealing," Clyde speculated. He reached into his pocket, pulling out an ancient, polished blade. "Or do you?"

It was a knife. *The* knife, the one he used on Rowley, on Darla. I stood up straight.

"I was thinking about ending you the first moment I laid eyes on you, but then I got to thinking," Clyde went on, studying his reflection in the blade. "Why not see what he knows? Any information you gathered was surely passed on to those friends of yours." He looked back at me. "I'll have to kill them of course. I caused several accidents this month already but hell, why not? There are so many strange incidents this time of year."

That was it. I couldn't take it any longer. I leaped to the left, trying my best to get around Clyde, but not before getting in a good punch first. He jumped around to block my exit, and in that second I knew I had lost. In the air, I could see the grin grow on his face. In a flash, I was pulled back, thin but powerful arms gripping me around the chest. I struggled, kicked, but it was no use.

"I knew you'd lead me to them," Clyde smiled, walking toward me. We had ended up with my back to the desk. Alder stood behind me stiff and strong. "That's why I kept you around. I knew those friends of yours would come find you. They're on their way right now, I believe." He checked his watch, "So much fresh spirit. I'll make a profit from you yet."

I struggled, glaring at him.

"Wipe that look off your face," Clyde chided. In one motion he sent a hand across my face, sending my head shooting to the left. It hurt, it hurt like something set me on fire. I had absolutely no memory of pain, no idea what it felt like. This was a wakeup call. It brought it all back to me.

"You really do have to be stubborn, don't you?" Clyde sighed to himself, shaking his head. "It would be so much easier if we could work together."

I felt something drip off my face. It felt like a drop of sweat, rolling down my cheek and off onto the floor. It was a glowing, white liquid that was just barely transparent. It held the essence of what a ghost on TV looked like, glowing and floating. It was a part of me, the part that kept me in purgatory.

Blood. Ghost blood.

"Why couldn't you be like our other friend, Rowley," Clyde went on. "Better manners. Maybe he'll convince your friends. He's the one taking them, after all."

I snarled at him. "Liar!"

"Call me what you want," Clyde smiled, plunging the dagger right through my skull.

Chapter 36

I was running. My feet hit the hard ground. The wind pushed against my face and brushed through my hair. I was panting, sweating, feeling my heart beat with every step and muscles bend at every command. I was alive, and I was running.

The streets of Chicago rushed past me as I ran. They were the streets I used to get to school. They were the streets where I had grown up. This was my town, my home, and I knew it well.

I wasn't thinking about that as I ran. I wasn't thinking about what a blessing it was to breathe, to feel, to know. I was running for my life that day. Unfortunately I didn't know how short that life would be.

Panting, I reached into my jacket with one hand while the other continued to pump at my side. I pulled out a phone, and with a jerky thumb began to dial a familiar number.

"I'm not here right now, leave a message," the voice on the other end recited.

"Sarah," I said, rounding a corner and dodging a group of dog walkers, "don't call me back. Delete this after you get it. I can't talk for long. I have to get away. I have to lie low for a bit."

I was getting tired, a stitch forming in my side. Talking wasn't helping me run any faster, but I had to do it. I had to tell the others.

"I think I broke a few more laws back there, sorry." I had been spying. I had been spying on things I wasn't supposed to see. And I got

caught. "I found out the Reaper, where he's staying, everything. He saw me after one of his rituals. He'll want me dead, Sarah."

The crossing ahead of me turned red. I couldn't stop there, not so close to the streets. I had no idea if the Reaper would send cars or people, but I knew for sure he would send something. I was out in public, but I wasn't safe. The Reaper was desperate. I turned down an alley.

"All we need is a name. Write everything down and destroy this message. Then get rid of your phone. I'm dead serious. This is all a lot bigger than we ever thought."

We were kids. We thought we could just figure things out on our own and could never get hurt. Life wasn't like that. We were all very, very mortal.

"It's the other ghosts. He's using them, that's how he does it! He uses the other spirits like some— some— I don't even know."

Something rustled in the dumpster nearby. I ignored it.

"But he extracts this stuff, like physical white stuff. I don't know what to call it. He uses it to make himself immortal."

Almost at the end of the alley, I could soon find a place to disappear from there.

"I'll tell you more when I find you," I went on. *"But get rid of your phone, I mean it. I don't want you to get any more involved in this. I love you."*

I was at the end of the alley. There was no sign of anything so far. I just might be safe.

"*To get his name, look up the place he works. It's—*"

Someone stepped out from the corner. I screeched to a halt and in shock dropped my phone to the ground. Alder. He raised his hand, and the last thing I saw was a flash of silver and the splatter of my own blood.

Chapter 37

The memory was gone as quick as it had come. And I was back, wherever that was.

There was pain. So much pain. I felt the white stuff, the ghost blood, gush out of my head and spill onto the floor. My head felt as if it was shattering, breaking into a million pieces and then by some curse squished back together again. My body screamed, sharing the pain of the head with a cry of agony. Clyde was unrelenting. He twisted the knife, pushing for more and more blood as he exacted his revenge. This is what he'd wanted from the moment he saw me. This is what he'd planned to do all along.

I don't know how long he made me suffer. It could have been seconds, it could have been hours. When he finally pulled the knife out it sent a whole new wave of pain. I fell to the floor instantly.

My vision was shaky, two split rooms in front of me shaking and swirling around. Clyde said something to someone, I couldn't hear what or to whom. I didn't know what was going on. It felt as if I were sinking through the floor. I might have been moving or I might have been standing still; it all felt the same to me. There was a high pitch ringing in my ears, or maybe a low whistle.

Something lifted me up. It was either Alder or Clyde or some figment of my imagination. It carried me to something, a closet or a bottomless pit. I was thrown in, and the door shut. I was left in darkness, as my whole world crumbled around me.

~

I saw a lot of things in that closet. I saw Sarah sitting on the bleachers by herself freshman year. Then I was four again, at my father's funeral. It was the first time in my life I took an interest in my sight. I saw the old pictures my grandma had in her apartment. They were of her friends, dead friends, the ones that came to dinner but didn't eat. Memories floated by of spirits pacing by their graves, sometimes giving me time to speak with them. I saw myself in the hospital with my grandma as a child, terrified by the number of the dead surrounding her.

I saw the book, Lyly, Rico, and my life spin through my mind. One memory would drift into another, each feeling the same. They were all there, every single moment of my past life, but they came out of order in a random, endless film montage with an audience of one.

I don't know if I was talking to myself. Rowley's rant was beginning to make sense, or at least becoming understandable. I couldn't remember what I had said, or how I had said it. Somebody had screamed at one point, or maybe that was me. Things in the closet seemed to be alive, watching me suffer.

The scenes before me showed my past life. All except one. The words Rowley had spoken to me echoed in and out at various times, beating into my head like the heart I didn't have.

"That one thing you have to do, or someone you have to say goodbye to."

I knew what that one thing was now. I watched my past, watched an angry kid plot for years on end. The Reaper. The Reaper. It was all about the Reaper. This was the task I set out to accomplish the moment I had realized who had killed my father. I had to find the Reaper. I had to kill him.

"Good to see you my boy!"

The words didn't have a connection to my memories. They didn't fit in, didn't make sense. I listened.

"Take a seat. You're looking better today."

No, that had nothing to do with my past life. What were the words doing here? What was going on?

"The money? On its way of course. Where are your friends?"

There was only a black void. No, not black, *dark*. I wasn't in a void. It was *dark*, because I wasn't at a funeral or high school. I was here, in a closet.

My head hurt. My core ached. The spot where I had been stabbed throbbed in a way no living body ever could. I felt so drained, my energy gone like I had run a thousand miles.

Only this time, the energy wasn't coming back. It couldn't be replenished because it had been stolen from me, taken.

But why was I here? Everything hurt so badly, it was hard to focus.

"They're waiting for me somewhere else." A voice said. It was a different voice, a voice I knew from before. But it wasn't from my memories.

"But Rowley," Clyde went on. "I thought we agreed on this."

"No," he cut in, his voice rising a bit. "No we didn't. I don't remember anything about what happened after— you know."

"Well," Clyde replied, a little more sternly, "you promised me."

"Where's DG?"

DG. Dead Guy. I was more than a dead guy now. I was Lucas West, and I had to get out of here. Rowley was right outside the door, a mere few feet from where I stood. I tried to sit up but my spirit didn't seem to be responding. It was at that moment I realized I couldn't move. I couldn't move my limbs, I couldn't open my mouth, and I couldn't speak. How was I supposed to get out?

"Your friend is in a bit of a predicament," Clyde explained. "He was able to recover his memories yesterday."

"What?" Rowley broke in. His tone seemed to brighten. "That's great! How did he do it?"

"Unfortunately," Clyde went on, not taking note of the ghost's words, "he has come to terms as the son of John West."

Rowley was silent for a moment. "Oh."

"Our friend DG has left us, I'm afraid," Clyde finished solemnly. "He does not require our assistance any longer."

"But DG wouldn't do that," Rowley protested. "He wouldn't go off on his own like that. He knows West is flat out crazy."

Crazy? I guess Rowley had been fed the same crazy story I had. I struggled with my own mind, trying to force myself to move, call out from the closet. The concentration only made me feel more drained. I felt close to passing out again.

"DG has a stronger loyalty to his father than he does to us," Clyde agreed. "He now feels his destiny is to destroy everything we've worked for."

I could practically see Rowley shaking his head. "But that doesn't make sense."

"I think it's better if we forget the whole matter."

Forget me?!

"Can't you do something?" Rowley asked. "Send someone to talk to him?"

"DG has chosen his path, Rowley," Clyde said sternly. "He betrayed me, and he'll betray you. You can't trust what he says anymore."

Rowley was silent.

"I already have enough work on my hands," Clyde went on, "what with the money for your brother's tuition."

"I know," Rowley sighed, giving in.

"I know it's hard to believe. I could barely believe it myself, the way he went off," Clyde frowned, sighing at the false memory. "But you can't trust him."

"Right," Rowley repeated half-heartedly. "Can't trust him."

"Now about his friends," Clyde continued, and I could hear the creak of his chair as he leaned forward. "You said they were waiting for you somewhere?"

"Yeah," Rowley replied, not quite out of the bad mood. "They want me to find him for them."

The others. I had almost forgotten. Clyde would go after them too. Only this time he knew where they were, and nothing stood in his way. He'd kill them, all of them. And that wasn't the only bloodshed he was after.

Angry, I pushed myself to move. My ghost wasn't responding the right way. I forced my spirit, my energy, to make itself go forward.

"Well let's hope DG doesn't get to them first," Clyde urged. "I want you to bring them to me, have me explain what I've told you."

No, that couldn't happen. I tried, I went to force myself to move, when suddenly my jaw clenched.

"Go get them?" Rowley repeated unsure. "They really didn't want to come in here. They think something bad will happen."

Without any warning I lunged forward, thrusting myself into the door of the closet. No noise resounded, but something was happening. I kept going forward: into the closet door, through it.

"Trust me," Clyde smiled, "everything will be—"

The sudden light was blinding, sickening. I was in the office, the light from the window searing on my aching skin. I realized in that moment why ghosts preferred the dark. It took me a while to even tell what I was seeing. I was on the floor, rolled into an upright position with one shocked ghost and a furious businessman staring at me.

"DG!" Rowley smiled, half relieved and half nervous. "You're—"

But I kept going. Everything was happening so fast it was hard to keep track of it all. I wasn't sure how I was doing this, but I didn't stop in the office. I fell down, through the floor, through the next floor, and the one after that. Down, down, down. I didn't know how to stop it. I could fall through each floor of the building if I wasn't careful. I had to think, focus, undo what I had just done.

With a sudden thud, I was back on the ground again. I was face down on a hard tile floor, the lack of pain added to the rush making me stop to catch myself. I was back in the lobby of the building, the scene calm as ever. I rolled over and sat up, still in disbelief. How did I do that? Had I just now picked up this ability?

Rowley said it was experience that allowed ghosts to move through objects. He could go through anything, fly around too. But it wasn't his experience, it was weakness. Rowley had had more blood taken than me.

Besides that, Rowley was with Clyde. He could follow me any second. He *would* follow me. I could explain myself once he got here. Then there was Alder. He could also get down here quickly. The guy was probably on his way. It was only a matter of seconds. I tried to stand, but my legs felt stiff and wiggly at the same time.

Desperately, I crawled toward the glass entrance. There was no chance I was making it out this door. But I needed to find the others, warn the others. Or would that lead Clyde straight to them? Either way, it wasn't good to stay here any longer than I had to. If I could just make it down the street.

Something dropped out of the ceiling. A black figure sunk like a bullet, landing perfectly on his own two feet. Alder was in front me, silent and just as deadly. As he looked down I saw my own pale reflection in his dark sunglasses. I made that face twist into a snarl. But Alder had me. There was no way I was getting out of this.

"Murderer," I glared up at him, kicking out. It was a weak attempt to trip him, but his feet stayed frozen to the ground. Alder remained right where he was, watching me as I tried to stand. I didn't understand why he was waiting. Why didn't he just end me?

"I hope it's worth it," I went on, looking him straight in the face. Alder's expression remained motionless. "I hope the money is worth every single soul you torture." The wound in my head was still fresh, fresh enough. "Enjoy the blood."

With a mere cough I hacked a mouthful of it, spitting it into Alder's face.

A hand came up. I didn't flinch, I wouldn't allow myself to. Maybe I was expecting more pain. But that was Alder's style. It didn't come. He gripped the front of my jacket. In a fraction of a second, the world was black again.

Chapter 38

I have to say, it was almost embarrassing to have gotten caught that easily. I didn't even remember what Alder had done, but I can tell you that that ghost was quick. When I woke up, I was glad I wasn't back in the closet. All I could say was I was in a different room. I wasn't even sure if I was in the building. There wasn't any pain, nothing like I had felt with the knife. But I opened my eyes only to find a hard pounding in my head.

The light was blinding. I didn't think that was possible, considering my situation. But it was real, pain and all. Was I dead? Like, legitimate, *dead* dead?

"Hey."

I forced my eyes open. The light hurt, but I made myself get used to it. The room could soon be recognized as a storage closet, a large one with metal racks and cardboard boxes. I was sitting in the corner, thrown in the back like a dead body. Not that the idea was far-fetched.

As the world adjusted around me, the words slowly came out. "What are you doing here?"

Rowley was in the middle of the room. Not quite sitting, but his legs were bent and he was hovering a few feet above the floor. He looked different. Not like the frantic kid at the house, but something was definitely there.

"Hi," he said again, almost sheepishly. He flashed a half-hearted grin. I frowned.

"Clyde put you here, didn't he?" I questioned. If he thought Rowley would change my mind, he was dead wrong. "You're still on his side."

"No! Well, let's just take it easy," Rowley protested, flying up with his hands held out defensively. He actually looked offended. "It's just, there's a lot going on with your life and stuff."

"Why am I here?" I asked. I didn't need Rowley here to convince me anything. "What's going on?"

"Just let me explain," Rowley insisted. There was sadness in his eyes I had never seen before. I folded my arms.

"You were with him the whole time, weren't you?"

"I know you're upset," he started. His eyes looked at the ground, then at me, then back to the ground. "I know you're mad cause your dad is on the other side. But just think for a sec. I don't want to have to leave you in here."

"You don't understand what's happening, do you?" I asked. "Clyde's not on the 'good side.' He's not on anyone's side. He only wants the dead for himself. And don't think you can come in here and change my mind!"

"Let me explain!" he sighed, looking down. He continued to talk, staring at the ground. "I didn't know about any of this, I swear. About you and your dad. I never wanted to stop you or anything. I just thought you were like any other newbie. We were just hanging out, you know?"

"But you kept things from me," I pointed out. "You let me get locked up in here. You knew about the knife."

"You messed with the system!" Rowley cried, throwing his arms in the air. "You don't mess with the system, DG. Nobody does. That's when things start going wrong, and nobody wants anyone to get hurt."

"Is that what they told you before they took the blood?" I demanded.

Rowley looked hurt. He stopped before he answered, looking away from me. "I don't know."

"They're killing us," I explained softly. I brought a hand to my chest, where the death wound would have been. "Body *and* spirit. How are you ok with that?"

Rowley was frowning at the ground. He looked back up at me. "You don't get it, DG. They're just some things we have to make sacrifices for."

"Like me?" I asked. "What am I giving up? Who am I giving up for? He just wants the blood."

"And I just want my family to be safe," Rowley exclaimed. "I didn't ask him to kill you. I didn't know! I never expected any of this."

"Well, then you just don't get it," I snapped. "All you ever thought about was yourself. I was trying to help people. I wanted to bring Clyde to justice. I was acting for my father, for the dead. All the things you obviously don't care about."

Rowley was angry now. He flew closer to me. "DG, wait."

I stood up, inches away from him. "My name's Lucas."

Whatever he was about to say, he stopped. We were eye to eye now. It was at this point we simultaneously knew in our hearts we couldn't be friends anymore. Maybe we never were. We were on opposite sides now.

"You messed with the system," Rowley finally muttered. "It's your own fault."

"Fine," I retorted. "What're you gonna do about it?"

"You're already dead," Rowley huffs, "it doesn't matter."

"Is that really what you think?" I demanded. "We don't matter? That you have to sell yourself to matter? Do you think that because you're dead your own family thinks you don't matter?"

"This isn't about me," Rowley hissed coldly. "Shut up."

"I would if you would actually listen," I protested. "They're gonna hurt me again. They're gonna hurt Cleo, and Sarah, and Rico. And they'll hurt you too. They'll hurt you through William's college tuition, and when he needs a job, and when he has debt."

"This isn't about that!" Rowley insisted. "I'm trying to stand for something here."

"Well I am too!" I cut in. "I had a life. I didn't know it was there, but now I do and I'm gonna fight for it. I'm gonna fight until I leave this planet. It's what I'm here to do."

As the words came out, I realized they were true. No matter what Rowley did, this was my last wish. This was my key out of purgatory.

"Then I guess we're on different sides then," Rowley concluded, drifting away.

I gave a stiff nod. "If you think you're gonna stop me."

"Well," Rowley insisted, floating farther and farther toward the door, "I do. For Will."

I nodded. "Fine."

"Fine," Rowley replied softly. He drifted out the door, and I was alone again. Come to think of it, maybe I always was.

Chapter 39

It was only when Rowley left that I took the time to look around the room. Probably because I didn't want to think about what just happened. The dimly lit closet was packed with boxes and carts full of bottles, but I hadn't taken the time to examine at them. Each one of the miscellaneous bottles and containers held a tiny, legible label.

Marie Ann: 24oz.

Josh Grover: 30oz

I continued on, looking through each of the bottles. On the few clear ones, I could see a white, milky liquid swirling around. I frowned, wondering what it could be when it hit me—

Ghost blood. This whole closet was full of ghost blood, each labeled by spirit. Shocked, I immediately went to the most recent cart.

Rowley Hart: 56oz

Lucas West: 15oz

That was me! *My* blood was stored in a bottle like a glass of milk. What did Clyde need all this blood for? Curious, I turned away from the bottles and pressed my hand to the wall. Nothing happened. How was I able to go through walls before, but not now? I pushed against it using my shoulder, digging into the floor with my heels to throw some more weight. It was no use, whatever had happened before seemed to be a fluke.

I backed up, putting myself a good distance from the wall and charged, running straight into the layer of cement in front of me.

I ended up on the ground, still stuck in the same old storage closet. Why did it work before? I had been weak, more flimsy. Now I was almost back to my old self. My core had recovered. I was still weak, much weaker than before. Still, I was strong enough to be kept inside these walls. I shuddered for a moment. I could only think about how much blood Rowley must have lost.

I needed to get out of here, to the others. We had to make a move on Clyde before he finished whatever he needed all this blood for.

"I've narrowed it down to three investors. I'll let them fight amongst themselves for the time being."

It was Clyde's voice. I looked around, but of course he was nowhere in the room. I spied an air vent in the corner, something that could be the source of the noise. I went closer.

"The bidding war and anticipation will create a high demand," he went on, "a higher profit."

Alder was next. His voice was closer in distance to Clyde's. "I don't think we can trust these potential buyers. What if they go public?"

"I've told each buyer we were working on a new drug," Clyde explained. "They understand this deal needs to stay under wraps"

"And what of the children?"

He was talking about the others. I pressed my ear to the vent.

"They can't be far from this building, if they've even left," Clyde replied. "I'm sure we can deal with them the same way we dealt with the first. They know too much after all. But on the bright side," there was a hint of a smile in his voice, "We may have more blood on the market."

There was a pause in the steady sound of footsteps. "What do you mean?"

"They're quite psychic," Clyde thought with a smile in his tone. "The gifted have the most powerful blood."

"Just how much blood do we need?" Alder rebuked. "Do we want the whole town to be after us for murder?"

The conversation took a small break, as if Clyde was considering what Alder had said. "I'll make note," he decided, "though I'm sure any of them could manage a very worthy payment."

I pulled away, shocked. I knew Clyde was a killer, but now that he was selling blood, he'd have even more motivation. He'd kill Cleo, Rico, and Sarah.

I had to get out of here. I looked around, frantically searching for a way. I charged blindly into a wall, hoping I'd get through. I went through aisles of boxes, searched for a door.

I heard a bump. I turned.

"Shhhhh!"

That definitely wasn't Alder, or Clyde. It wasn't Rowley either, not that I cared. Still, I cocked my head, walking toward the door.

"Lucas?"

I ran over, pressing my ear to the door.

"Guys?"

"I told you!" Cleo triumphed in a loud whisper.

"Ok fine, but it's locked," Rico pointed out.

"I'm not going in. I feel something awful in there."

"How do we get in?"

"Anyone gotta bobby pin?" Sarah asked.

"Are you serious?"

"Guys, guys, I can hear you," I cut in with my own whisper, still listening through the door. How did they get up here? It was a free building, but someone should've spotted them by now.

"Even he can hear us. You guys need to be quieter," Sarah pointed out.

"Shh!" Rico hissed sarcastically. There was more rustling, this time from the door knob. Even with my memories back, I had forgotten how often we used to sneak around like this. But we couldn't pick a lock, not without bringing to proper equipment.

"Guys, it's ok," I managed. "You won't be able to get me out of here and Clyde's looking for you. How'd you find me?"

"That other dead guy left us," Rico said, coming to stand closer, "so we thought this was more of a do-it-yourself situation."

"Lucas," Cleo started, "what's in there? It feels— I'm picking up something horrible."

"It's ghost blood. There's a lot of—never mind that." I pressed my hand against the door. "You guys need to get out of here."

"And go where?" Rico asked, the same time Sarah said, "We're not leaving you."

I looked at the door. They were right there, just on the other side of this piece of wood. Yet this piece of junk was enough to separate us.

"He can't hurt me." That was a lie, kind of. "Not like the way he can hurt you. He wants you dead, do you hear me? He'll kill you if you stay here."

There was silence on the other side of the door. Sarah spoke up. "Then what are we supposed to do?"

"Get the cops," I reasoned. "Get anyone. Say someone's gonna die. Tell them there are drugs in here. Just get a lot of living people here and fast."

"Will do," she replied. I heard the sound of shuffling. The others were leaving, quickly. But there was a gentle thump from the other side of the door. Sarah was pressing her hand on the door. I knew she was.

"We'll see you soon Lucas."

I felt cold. I pressed my hand harder into the door, as if I could reach back to her. "I'll see you soon."

Chapter 40

I listened until the very last echo of their footsteps was gone. My ears soon filled with a dull achy silence, longing for the voices that had once hung in the air. Yet I knew my longing didn't matter. They were safe, and that was all I could ask for.

I stepped away from the door, turning back to the shabby storage room. I had to find a way out of here. I walked the perimeter of my cramp quarters, trying to determine the possible number of exits. There was the air vent, but I already knew I couldn't squeeze through that thing. Of course there was the door. I had already tried pounding on it for ten minutes. That thing wasn't going to bust even if I had the strength of a living person. So my only option left was passing through the walls. There were no other windows, holes or skylights to work with.

Again, I had already tried that. Pressing myself against the wall, I closed my eyes and concentrated. I tried to feel weightless, like I had after I was stabbed. Yet no matter how much I tried I was just like the blood in the jars: hidden away and secure.

I was ramming myself against the wall when I heard footsteps again. Hearing the sound I came to a sudden halt. They were slow steps, the kind of a man with a great weight on his shoulders. They stopped at the door. I waited for the sound of keys, for the doorknob to click. But there was none. Instead, the man merely passed through the door.

I was caught in mid-run, my hands pressed against the wall I wished to pass through. Alder was neither impressed nor amused by my escape attempt. He simply gestured to the door with a jerk of his head.

"It's time to go."

I grew stiff. Instantly I was standing upright, hands curled into fists.

"I won't go. No with you."

Alder didn't reply. Instead he grabbed my arm, his iron grip pulling me toward the door, "Have it your way then."

We were forced out into the hall, Alder and I. We went from room to room, farther and farther from the bottle-filled closet I called a prison. I fought him the whole way, kicking and trying to free myself. Eventually he had both of my arms pinned behind my back, dragging me like he was taking out the garbage. I had walked through the walls this time. Again, maybe touching Alder had something to do with it. He was almost too solid for a skeleton man so thin, too strong. The blood has made him into some kind of monster.

The two of us ended up in an empty conference room. One long table took up almost the entire space, completed with two rows of chairs. The moment we were completely inside, he threw me against the wall. I crashed into it and slid to the ground, the ability to pass through objects lost. Even though it didn't hurt it was still humiliating. In three strides he was next to me, staring down with his nonexistent eyes.

"I'm feeling much better now," I challenged as I rolled to face him. "I'll fight you."

Alder glanced at the clock. "You have ten minutes." There was no reaction to what I said. "So you're going to listen to me so I only have to say this once." Out of everything Alder had ever said to me, this was his longest utterance. I was so surprised I didn't say anything for a moment. "Get up."

I stood up with hesitation. "What are you gonna do, huh?" I questioned with a glare. "Kill me? You already did that."

Alder cut me off. "Don't interrupt me." He was angry, but had no intention of using force.

"Why? What do I owe you?" I demanded.

Nothing in Alder's face changed. "Nine minutes."

"Give me *one* reason I shouldn't strangle you right now," I barked back.

"Because I'm giving you the chance to save your friends."

I stopped. With those bulky shades it was hard to tell if he was lying or not. Clyde was behind everything this ghost did. Alder would never give me an opportunity like that. Then again, Clyde and Alder had seemed to be arguing earlier. I decided I'd give him a chance, nodding to let him continue.

"Every death," he told me, "every killing has been for a designated purpose. Each victim we chose deserved to die, or they were close to death. You weren't part of that plan, and neither was your father."

Deserved to die? What gave Alder that right, judging who was to live?

"I'm sorry," he finally said.

I realized he was apologizing for my murder. "It's a little late for that," I interjected, frowning. If he hadn't been so eager to kill me in the first place, maybe it'd be different. But this guy killed my father, and me. Sorry wasn't going to cut it.

"I know," he stated, and I could hear the steely undertone. "But you should know that you and your father were the first— our first unrelated murders."

"And killing for your 'business' is ok?" I pointed out.

"I already explained that to you." Now he was getting frustrated. "Did it ever occur to you that we were helping that ghost of yours, that his family couldn't pay those medical bills?"

Rowley. I didn't bother mentioning we weren't the chummiest of friends at this point.

"And Darla," he went on, "the girl who had lost herself in purgatory. The one we attempted to help pass on before your father intervened."

I flinched. To claim my dad was the bad guy made me want to go at Alder again. But I controlled myself. My dad was already dead, but I could still help the others.

"You didn't have to hurt them," I pointed out. In my life I'd help a spirit once in a while, like Cleo had. Only we had never stabbed anyone.

"Clyde needs to sustain his life," Alder sniffed, staring down my insult. "You don't understand his situation."

"And I don't care," I spat. For someone complaining about the time, he sure took a while to get the point. "You said you would help me?"

Alder took a moment. I'd never seen him talk this much without Clyde by his side. Maybe he hadn't done it in years, decades. It must be hard on an old soul.

"We only took what we needed," he repeated, looking at the clock. Seven minutes.

"And when you drank blood?" I argued. "How much did you 'need?'"

That comment hurt Alder. His frown deepened. "Now Clyde wants to take even more, for profit. I never supported that decision."

It never occurred to me Alder had the guts to argue so much with Clyde. I thought of him as the bodyguard, silently at his side. Now he spoke as his own person.

"Selling blood has corrupted him," he declared, looking back at me. "I think it may be time to end the operation."

I stared at him. Was he saying what I thought he was saying? From his perspective, that was as good as treason. I frowned, wondering if he was lying to me, stalling.

"How do I know you're telling the truth?" I asked.

Alder turned away. He moved slowly, the soul of an ancient man taking small steps.

"It was a long time ago, 1811. I was so much younger back then, so naïve. We both were. He had wanted to give life to others, and I had wanted to cheat death. We spent so much time looking for an answer, wasted so much time." Alder shook his head. "Clyde had the sight, that's how he learned about it. Do you remember how the Reaper got his weapon?"

I nodded.

"Then you know. He made the deal. He did it behind my back."

Alder almost looked sad, disappointed. He had no right to act so innocent. "You still went along with it," I cried. "You still killed all those people."

"You have to understand," Alder countered. "I was horrified by it. Never in my life had I agreed to use a contraption from the Devil."

That was a lie. "But you used it in the afterlife."

"You don't think I know that?" he snapped. "I sat by for thirty years while he used that weapon. For thirty long years he stayed as he was while the rest of us began to age. I was starting to change. I was becoming different, older. Clyde too began to change, but his was a different kind. He was getting stronger, faster. But with that came impatience, power, and a need for more."

"You could have left him," I suggested. "Clyde was immortal, you weren't. You should have left him."

Alder turned away. "I sometimes ask myself the same question. Clyde was my only friend, the only family I had left. Even then he was becoming a stranger to me. But I still cared for him, still feared for him. A mere knife wasn't going to change that. And I wasn't about to let Clyde fend for himself."

I didn't want to interrupt, but it seemed like Clyde was doing a fine time handling himself. Maybe Alder was afraid of what Clyde would turn into. Or maybe he wanted to see immortality in action. Either way, it was too late to change the past.

"But I gave in," he continued. "I couldn't let myself go any further. I wouldn't let myself die. Watch."

And before I could even flinch, Alder slammed his head into mine.

Chapter 41

Alder was standing in the back of a cabin in the evening twilight. He was alive. Though this Alder was the same age, he was almost unrecognizable. His hair seemed to stretch down the sides of his face and connect at the chin to form a mane-like beard. He was still thin, that seemed to be his general stature. But the skin that was now pale and lifeless had a colored glow to it, kissed by the sun. In addition, this Alder had something the current Alder declined to show: his eyes. They were a wide set and a deep wooden brown.

Across from him was Clyde Harrison. Besides the clothes and hair, this Clyde was exact the same one from upstairs in his office. The resemblance was eerie. Alder watched him Clyde light his pipe. He now looked more like Alder's son than his business partner. As the age gap widened they seemed to grow more distant, like strangers. Alder couldn't take it anymore. His time was running out, and he didn't want to lose any more of it.

"I want in."

Clyde seemed genuinely shocked. He turned to his partner, the pipe still in hand. "You will need the sight, like me."

"I understand."

Clyde pulled out the knife from his sheath, holding it out for his friend to see. "Are you sure?"

That was the only moment of hesitation Alder had. After that, any second was kept to himself.

"Of course."

There was pain. The ritual to gain the sight was something neither of them had ever attempted, much less thought about. Clyde's was a born gift; Alder's would be man-made. Of course the pain was brutal, Alder didn't expect anything less. But as the older man staggered to the ground, Clyde was more concerned about completing the ritual than his comrade's safety. Maybe it was the struggling victim, or maybe it was the determination of Clyde's hand. But it was an accident. Alder's memory couldn't have been clearer: it was an accident.

They had done it outside, a full moon shining through the trees. Something was different about Alder after the event, something he'd spend a century hiding from the world. Clyde tried to give Alder the sight the only way he knew how. His eyes had been cut off with the knife.

They were gone. The sockets were completely empty now, dried brown lines trailing down his cheeks. His ghost looked just like the Alder of today, one in different clothing. Maybe he had died of blood loss, or maybe he couldn't take the pain anymore. Either way, Alder was dead.

Slowly, ever so slowly the new ghost raised his hands to his face. They were still good hands, the hands of a man in his mid-sixties. Alder had no eyes yet he could see. Hesitantly, he traced the outline of his own sockets. Clyde stood a few feet away, watching in sheer horror. Alder had gotten his wish. He wouldn't age any more.

"Alder, I am so sorry," Clyde stammered. He was grief-stricken, shock and sorrow taking over his features. "I never meant for this to happen." For the first time ever Clyde looked so lost, something inside him broken. He continued to stammered, his voice weak, "I am so, truly, sorry."

He dropped the knife, his hands and the blade tainted with human blood. Next to the weapon, a figure was slumped over by a tree. Its head had dropped down to its chest, like a puppet without a master. Alder.

Horrified, the ghost fell to his knees. His hand still rested on his cheek, fresh blood mingled with his fingertips as he stared at his own corpse.

"My God."

Years went by, decades. Though Alder's clothes and looks may have changed, his face and stature remained the same. For the most part the two of them stayed together. Sometimes Alder would walk out for a few months, or vice versa. But they always came back. It turns out in a world of constant change, they were the only things that stayed the same.

It was modern times now, or at least it seemed to be. Clyde was doing some sort of paperwork. His hair was cut short, shorter than it was now. His clothes were also different. He had braces to correct his teeth. Still, he looked the exact same as he had almost 200 years before.

"I'm hungry Alder," Clyde said to his friend. He wasn't talking about food. Clyde was at his desk, different from his current one. This was one among many other cubicles, although there was no one around to overhear Clyde talking to himself. He must have been newly hired, just moved into this city. "I'm starting to feel it coming again."

Alder nodded. Clyde hadn't been himself this week. The past decade they discovered a few weeks without blood would exhaust him. The more years that passed, the more he needed to sustain himself. Clyde was rather irritable when he was hungry, something Alder didn't enjoy putting up with.

"I *need* one," he urged. He had to get Alder's approval for every victim. After all, he was the one that did the job. "One that won't leave like the others." He looked up at Alder. "Or something to hold me over for a few days."

"You'll find someone," Alder said patiently. The ghost never liked when Clyde's options were limited. Once, and only once, Alder allowed Clyde to use the knife on himself. But he had sworn he'd never give up his blood again. "That's the reason you took your job."

"But they're all so old," Clyde complained. He was shuffling through files of his clients. "The younger ones are a lot less work." He skimmed through the papers at his desk, each with a photograph and information on each person.

"What does it matter?" the ghost asked him. "They all have blood."

"It's a whole lot more than blood," Clyde sighed, opening his file for more papers. "We need someone to stick around for more than a few days, a willing customer." The words sounded so simple and clear when Clyde said them. But Alder knew exactly what that meant, and he hated it. "Maybe we can work out a system."

Alder thought about it. They usually found some spirit for a few days, a week at most. The alternative was to make a spirit. Clyde had been insisting on that more and more over the last twenty years. Alder was still unsure about it.

"If they are willing," Alder agreed. But no one would be, not without force.

"And willing they will be," Clyde smiled, his business smile broadening. He flipped through the pictures on his desk, finally stopping on one with the client waving at the camera. He pointed at the picture. "That one."

Alder leaned over to see the photo. He frowned, borderline disgusted. "That's a kid."

"A dying kid," Clyde urged. "Look at that. What's he got, a month left? I've had to go to the family's house a few times. His parents can barely afford me anyway."

The memory ended. Obviously Alder didn't want me to see the rest, spare me the trouble of it. I didn't have to guess who the kid was. Rowley had told me he died in his sleep, that it was completely natural. But that wasn't true. Whether he knew it or not, Rowley had been murdered too.

Chapter 42

I had never been in a memory so long. I had forgotten about the present-day Alder that now stood before me. He took a few steps back, watching my reaction. I was surprised by how concerned he looked, like he actually cared about me. This was the same man that had killed my father, the one that had killed me. Not to mention all the countless others, including Rowley. I wouldn't let myself forget that.

"You can fill in the blanks," he finished.

"Like when you killed me?" I asked. Alder gave no reply. Yet I knew behind those glasses he could not meet my eye. "How did you kill Rowley?"

"Slipped something in his IV," Alder stated. "He was asleep. Never saw it coming."

"It started with him, didn't it?" I questioned. "Then you got more and more spirits until you became what you are now."

"Against my wishes, if you haven't noticed," Alder pointed out.

"But you went along with it," I countered. "You didn't do anything to stop it."

"I know," he admitted. There was a bitter, regretful tone was in his voice. "What I did is done."

I remembered he had promised to help me, to save my friends. That almost, *almost* gave me a reason not to yell at him. Almost.

"So what?" I demanded. "You said you'd help."

Alder reached into his suit jacket. It didn't take me any time to realize what he'd pulled out: the knife.

"I quit my job, Lucas," he sighed. I pulled back, waiting for the bodyguard to grab me again. To my surprise, he didn't attack me. He didn't move. Instead, he reached up, removing his sunglasses. The same black, blank sockets bored into my eyes just like before. Ghosts didn't need eyes to see. He could've healed over the years, made himself look like he used to. But he hadn't. He had never forgotten what Clyde did. He had never moved forward. "I don't have a reason to fight you anymore."

Something was wrong. There was a strange look on the ghost's face. He looked oddly at peace for someone who re-lived so much. He swayed as if he were drunk. His mouth was quirked at an odd angle. It was the look of someone about to do something crazy.

"Alder stop." But it was like I wasn't there anymore. Alder kept talking, talking to himself.

"I tried to get fired before, but he wouldn't have it. He can't stand not to have his way."

He positioned the weapon, this time at his own head.

"Alder?" I said, bewildered. Some alarm was going off in my mind. I was afraid. "What are you doing?"

"There's only one way out of purgatory for me. Clyde made sure of that."

I watched, stunned and horrified. I felt stiff, like I couldn't move. If I tried, Alder would stop me.

Now his sockets met my eyes. "I'm letting you end the operation. Here's your chance."

Alder steadied himself, the point of the blade barely grazing the skin above his ear.

"You don't have to do this," I told him.

"No, Lucas," he told me, "I do. It's my time." A thought, maybe a memory, must have crossed his mind. He smiled. "Tell Harrison I'll see him again. In hell."

The knife smashed through Alder's skull. White ghost blood gushed from the spot, a lot cleaner than a living wound but twice as horrifying.

I jumped back, keeping myself away from the ridiculous amount of white blood. There was so much blood. I thought the pain would have made Alder struggle, but he did no such thing. He was strong. He had forced the knife in deeper, working to cut through his entire brain. He continued to stand perfectly still, that same smile still touching his lips.

I could watch the blood wash away Alder. He grew more faded and blurry, like the color being sucked from a painting. The very hand clenching the knife soon dropped the weapon, and the blurry spirit lurched forward like a puppet with cut strings.

In a matter of seconds, Alder's body had faded. It wasn't a big phenomenon, nothing like Rowley had made it out to be. He simply went still, like his very core had been wrung dry.

Then he was gone. There was no outline or something proving he was once there. He was just gone. It was over, and I'd never see him again. Would I?

All that was left was the knife. Without much hesitation I picked it up and slipped it into my pocket. No good letting it fall into the wrong hands, right?

I looked back down the conference room. The door opened, and some businessmen filed in. They made small talk as they entered, completely oblivious to what just happened. They didn't know a man had passed on ten feet from where they stood. No one did. And despite all that man had done to me it still felt wrong. Someone, anyone should be here to remember what Alder had lived for.

But there wasn't. There was just me.

I stepped back from the scene, a hand coming to my own throat. I had to go. I had to protect the others. But I couldn't just leave, could I?

Time answered for me. I scampered out the door before the last man came in, squeezing through as the door was shut. I was now in a long hallway, one that I knew from the times I've spent in it. Knife still concealed I took off toward the office, the one I had been to so many times before. There was only one person left to face, the person who had killed my father and ordered to have my life taken. And that man was Clyde Harrison.

Chapter 43

I crept my way towards Clyde's room. This time there was nothing the man could threaten me with. By now I could only hope Sarah and the others were far away from the Reaper as possible. It was just me and him.

I arrived as I had so many times before. The door was ajar, and I helped myself into the office. The place was empty. Maybe Clyde had gone looking for Alder. Wouldn't he be surprised. I made my way forward, unsure of myself as I made my way to the desk. Would I wait here for Clyde to get back? This was too easy. Something wasn't right.

"Hello Lucas."

I jumped, whirling around to see Clyde standing in the entrance. He was cool and confident, business smile as broad as ever. I stood my ground, staring him down with my feet firmly planted. I met his face with my own look of hatred. There was no use backing out of this now.

Our positions were reversed. I was standing behind the desk now, and Clyde was just making his way in. That didn't seem to faze him though.

"Have a seat champ." He gestured to his oversized desk chair. I remained where I was.

I decided to speak. "Alder's gone. I'm not doing anything for you."

Clyde smile fumbled. It wasn't fear that took over his features. For a moment, he looked dejected, maybe even a little sorry.

"Have it your way," Clyde sighed, stepping inside the office. He locked the door behind him.

The sliver of emotion he had shown was quickly covered up. Clyde was too collected, almost too calm. He had lost his number one ally, yet he wasn't the least bit sorry? What kind of game were we playing?

"Have I complimented you on your blood yet?" Clyde inquired, cocking his head at me. I shook my head. "Well then I must say so! It's quite strong. I got quite the fortune for it. But you knew about that already, didn't you?"

He chuckled at the idea while I remained where I was. "Alder said you shouldn't be selling blood."

Clyde stopped laughing, now rigid. His smile was starting to look like a snarl. "I have to sell blood, don't you understand that? This job is distracting me from work. I don't need these clients anymore. And I have to make money don't I?" He paused briefly, his efforts to be collected less and less effective. "You don't have to be so old fashioned, Lucas. Can't you see why I have to do this? Why it's necessary?"

My forehead creased. "I don't think it's ever necessary to kill someone."

"And where has that brought you?" he jeered, gesturing with his hands. This was a real laugh, a cruel one. "Survival of the fittest, my boy."

Survival was second nature to Clyde Harrison. He strode forward, leaning on the desk now.

"Fortunately, you still have some tricks up your sleeve." He smiled at me. "You have very powerful blood, Lucas. I'd love to harness that power."

"I don't care," I cut in. "Why not just get rid of me now then? Get it over with!"

"Lucas," he pulled back chuckling, like he was explaining a joke, "I'm not going to get rid of you. No! You're too valuable."

"Alder's moved on," I went on. "And I'm the reason you have no right hand man."

He paused. I expected this comment to take an emotional hit, but Clyde didn't show it. "Yes, yes you are," he finally nodded. "It was unfortunate. But *very* impressive."

I stared him down. "What do you want?"

Clyde walked to my side of the desk, stopping in front of me. I waited for him to strangle me or something, but he stood with his hands clasped together.

"Do you mind?"

He wanted his desk. I stepped back and allowed him to open a drawer. Clyde knelt down and started rummaging through his belongings. Although I tried to see what he was doing I couldn't get a clear view. I could only assume whatever it was had to be dangerous. I tensed up, ready to fight. Instead Clyde set something down on the table: a bottle.

"Have you ever had blood, Lucas?" Clyde asked casually. "It's quite the pick me up, you know. It's what made Alder so strong."

I blinked, suddenly nervous and afraid. I realized where this was going.

"Don't tell me you haven't been curious," Clyde questioned with false surprise. "I know, I *guarantee* it will do great things for you."

In a flash, Clyde tossed the bottle to me. I was so surprised that I automatically caught it. I turned the container to face me, surprised I could even hold it. It was because of the blood inside; I could feel it. It swished it around, white and pure. It wasn't mine but another's that was inside, probably someone I didn't know.

I suddenly got a weird feeling in my stomach, one I remembered but had never felt since my death: hunger.

"You are twice the man Alder ever was before his first shot," Clyde remarked to me, and I knew he meant it. "A powerful psychic makes a powerful poltergeist."

I looked back at the bottle. I knew I could uncap it, I knew I could drink it, all of it. The hole from the knife would be restored. I'd be whole again.

"We could do great things, Lucas," Clyde told me eagerly. "I need a new handyman."

I looked at the bottle. If I didn't drink it, Clyde could kill me right here. If I did, all those deals— all those people – their deaths would be on my hands.

"What," I stuttered, confused. "What about the business deals? Rowley? My friends?"

"I have hundreds of other clients," Clyde disclosed. "They can live forever if they want. I can grant favors. It's what I do."

I returned my gaze to the bottle. I wanted to drink it. My core knew I *should* drink it. I could be like Alder, move objects, be with Sarah. I held the bottle up to my face. What would happen after I drank it? Years from now, decades, would Clyde still be this friendly?

"I think," I started. But the sentence wouldn't finish itself. I couldn't stop watching the bottle. My mind went to Alder, dead for all those years. His last few words still echoed through my mind. I couldn't do it. I couldn't become what Alder suffered through. "I think he's right. You belong in hell!"

I threw the bottle on the ground with all my strength. It smashed to pieces, the liquid inside bubbling and vaporizing into the air. In a matter of seconds it was gone, vanished in the air. Clyde's eyebrows skyrocketed.

"What have you done?" he cried. "Do you know how much blood that was? Do you know how much it cost?"

He slammed his hands onto the desktop, making me jump. His eyes bored into mine with a look I can only describe as crazy. I pulled back, hair prickling on my neck. My body froze and I could only wait for Clyde's wrath to come at full force. But it didn't. He didn't say anything. Clyde Harrison took a deep breath.

"I gave you a chance, Lucas," Clyde cried, too angry to be diplomatic. "I gave you a chance to redeem yourself. But if that's your choice." He snarled at me, his eyes burning. "I'm afraid you can't be on this planet anymore."

Chapter 44

Without thinking, I pulled up my only defense. The knife was out of my pocket and in both hands, pointed straight at Clyde's heart. "Make one move and you're dead."

It was a little ironic, the dead killing the living. That's what had started this whole mess. Clyde watched the knife with a look of shock, then amusement. Finally he barked out a laugh.

"You don't have the guts," he sneered. He held out both arms. "Go ahead, do it."

I hesitated. Was this yet another one of Clyde's tricks? I gave the notion a second thought, just long enough for Clyde to snap forward, one hand getting a strong grip on the hilt of the knife. If I had drunk the blood, maybe I would have had a chance against the businessman. Now I didn't stand a chance. Our hands wrestled across the table, Clyde using his free one to wrench mine away. Within seconds, he had torn my only hope from my hands, raising it up in victory.

"I think I'll take care of this, thank you," Clyde sneered, already planning where to strike. I stepped back, reality sinking in. Without the knife, I was a *dead* dead man. My leaving wasn't a huge issue, but once I was gone, he'd go after the others. He'd kill Sarah and Rico. He'd take revenge against me on everyone I loved. "I'll be sure to tell all your friends how you died." His eyes flickered. "It'll be the last thing they will ever hear."

"Wait!"

Something swooped down on Clyde, so unsuspecting he was duped into having the knife snatched from his grasp. Rowley was in the air holding the knife up so high it practically hit the ceiling.

"You can't touch this," he yelled triumphantly, looking down on us.

I looked confused. "Rowley?"

"Rowley," Clyde said calmly as he held out his hand. "Give that back now."

"No way," he rebuked. "I'm not letting people die anymore."

"Rowley," I called, getting his attention. He looked over at me.

"You can't have it either," he insisted, waving it at me.

"I don't want it. Just get rid of it, ok?" He frowned, not sure whether to trust me or not. But whatever we had fought about didn't matter anymore. "Please."

"Don't you dare!" Clyde shouted, turning. "Get down here. I can *ruin* you *and* your family, do you understand?"

"Not if we ruin you first," Rowley replied, sticking out his tongue at Clyde. Our eyes met again, and he smiled. I smiled back. It the closest thing we had to an apology.

Rowley used his flight to his advantage. While Clyde swiped at the ghost Rowley managed to hold the knife away from him. Though Rowley could pass through walls he couldn't take the knife with him. He was stuck with us now, and as much in danger as I was.

"We've all been around long enough Clyde," Rowley said, a somber note in his voice, "haven't we? Don't you think it's been enough?"

"You don't understand," Clyde hollered, more and more angry. "I need that weapon!"

"Nobody needs to live forever," I cut in, stepping closer. "Get rid of it."

Rowley considered both prospects. "Well," he hesitated.

"Rowley!" Clyde snapped. "I'm asking you nicely."

Rowley looked from one face to the other. "Ok Clyde," he decided, flipping the knife in the air with a smirk on his face. "Let's make a deal."

Clyde didn't say anything, his eyes on the knife. He was prepared to make sacrifices, but he was not the type to grovel.

"I need more money," Rowley started, a wicked grin growing, "another eight— no, ten thousand dollars. Swear you'll do it!"

"You'll get nothing unless I receive that knife first," Clyde responded, fists clenching.

"What's that?" Rowley asked, cupping his ear. "I'm sorry, I can't hear you with all this traffic outside." He tapped the window with the tip of the weapon, slowly chipping through the window, "Pretty loud, don't ya think?"

"You'll stop this nonsense first if you want anything from me," Clyde responded, narrowing his eyes.

"Is it hot in here?" Rowley questioned. He put a hand to his chin in wonder. "I don't know. I've been dead for twelve years." This time he banged the knife against the glass, causing a definite crack. A hole sprouted from the tip of the blade. "How about a nice breeze?"

"Rowley," Clyde was starting to look pale, "you don't know what you're doing."

"Watch me," Rowley challenged back. He banged the knife again, and again, and again.

Smash! Rowley poked a giant hole in the window big enough for his head. Glass shattered down to the streets below. Rowley stuck his hand through the crack, dangling the knife over the edge.

"Now if you want this back," he started.

Clyde didn't wait for the rest. He lunged for the knife, shoving me aside and almost barreling through the window to get to it. Rowley reacted out of instinct and pulled away, the knife slipping through his hands. It fell barely two feet before Clyde grabbed it again.

"I think I'm done with you boys," he snarled to us. "I'm afraid I'll have to take another payment!"

He stepped back with the knife in his hand. A harsh hunger for vengeance gleamed in his eyes, ready for the kill. His hair was ruffled and his tie was crooked. He had lost the appearance of the well-to-do citizen he pretended to be. Rowley and I both jumped forward, tackling him simultaneously. Clyde crashed against the window, head making an alarmingly loud *crack*. The office shook, a filing cabinet crashing to the floor and landing on Clyde's legs. With its help, we were able to pin him down, each of us holding an arm.

"You don't understand," Clyde said again, kicking against us holding him down. "This was made for me. I *need* it. Give it to me!"

"Sorry boss," Rowley breathed, wrenching the knife from Clyde's grasp. "Deal's off."

A corner of my mouth turned up. "You do the honors."

Rowley took back the murder weapon, arching his arm back to throw it. "*Bon voyage.*"

With his last burst of strength, Clyde kicked off the cabinet. He threw me off his arm, hysterically pulling himself to his feet. "Don't!"

But it was too late. Rowley had already thrown the knife, his perfect aim sending it through one of the holes in the window. Clyde bolted after it, desperation clear in his eyes. He would have caught it too, if he hadn't stumbled.

I'm not sure what he tripped on; I'm not even sure if Clyde knew or even cared. How it happened, no one would ever be completely sure. But what occurred next would be known forever. Clyde Harrison fell into the window.

The cracks through the window had been spreading, growing like a spider web through the whole struggle. Every bang and bump during the fight had aided his downfall. As Clyde fell, he grabbed the closest thing he could find. And the worst part was he didn't let go.

Clyde fell into the window. He fell *through* the window. And he took me with him.

Chapter 45

The sound of breaking glass was crystal clear. It's a sound that will never leave my mind. Clyde crashed through the window, scattering glass everywhere. We fell toward the unforgiving ground, one that was thirty-one stories below.

Rowley watched, his mouth open. The floating ghost rapidly shrank smaller and smaller as we sunk downward. The Reaper fell face up, unable to catch his breath or scream. Clyde's face was a gasp of sheer terror. I couldn't get away from him. His grip on my shirt was like stone.

I turned toward the ground. It was rushing toward us at a terribly rapid speed, much too fast for comfort. I looked at Clyde, whose glassy eyes locked onto mine with a look of dead hatred. In that moment, maybe the final moment of his life, he hated me with all his being.

We hit the ground.

The impact didn't affect me. It was the second time I had fallen out of a window as a ghost, and hopefully it would be my last. I stood up, wiggling from the loosened grip and stumbling a safe distance away. To my knowledge, the ordeal was finally over. But what did that mean?

The dust cleared. Clyde Harrison was lying face up on the ground. His body had been smashed in the most awkward angle. I had expected him to be crushed, but what I saw was much worse.

One of his hands was flung in my direction, five uncurled fingers reaching in my direction. But the hand had lost its will. Red, living blood oozed from various cuts, dripping from his exposed cracked ribs. His body was limp, like a puppet with cut strings. He was staring up into the sky, looking at the sun he could no longer see. His skull was sunken and destroyed. The man's eyes were open and blank, something like horror in them. His slacked jaw was unmoving.

He was dead.

I backed up, not daring to look away. The wild panic of the fall still coursed through my veins. Surely a man so powerful, a man with so many allies, a man as great as Clyde Harrison, the Reaper, couldn't die so easily. He must have been faking it, or had a back-up plan, or was waiting for the proper moment. But I waited and the truth slowly sank in. Alder *was* his backup plan, and Alder was long gone. Clyde Harrison was really dead.

"Lucas?" Rowley's voice rang out unsurely. He was floating down to my side, his face a mixture of shock and fear. I turned to him, his bright green eyes wide and intense. "Is he?"

"Yeah," I replied. "He is."

It was unnaturally quiet for such a traumatic event. We stood as still as the air itself. I couldn't believe what our eyes were telling us. A man who had given his soul to feast on the dead had finally joined them. And now, so many spirits had finally been avenged.

Out of the corner of my eye I noticed something on the ground. It was the knife, silver and glistening in the sunlight. Without alerting Rowley I crept over and picked it up. It felt dull and weightless in my hands. I slipped it in my pocket, heading back to Rowley. He too said nothing, but gave a nod of approval.

It didn't feel like it happened. I didn't get any relief out of the death. Or regret, come to think of it. I didn't kill this man. That was his own doing.

"Rowley," I said, turning to him. "We can go home."

But we didn't move. We watched the body, still as stone. People were beginning to notice now. A few had gathered in wonder a distance from the body like they had from my own when I had died. Somebody would call 911. Clyde Harrison would be taken away. In a matter of days, he would be six feet underground.

Something moved. An untouched hand, a dead hand, twisted. New fingers, old fingers, ripped through the dead flesh, craning and stretching toward the sky.

"NO."

The sound was cold, inhuman. We watched, horrified as Clyde Harrison ripped away from his own body. The mangled hand tore through the skin of its host and dug into the cement with its cracked, bleeding nails. Another hand followed, and in the next moment, the ghost had pulled himself through his corpse.

His face was old, the face of a man who should've died long ago. Withered and shrunken, the remnants of a businessman soon came to stand, blood mangled in his torn clothes. The whites of his eyes were black, sunken in to make his face look like a skull. He was no ordinary spirit. He was a nightmare.

"You took my empire," the thing howled, its voice cracked from the rustic grave. "My life's work! I won't stand for it."

I'd never seen a ghost so inflicted, so diluted as the one standing in front of me. He was strong too. I could see the energy, the blood, float off him like steam. He still had the power he had stolen from the dead. He could still use it as his own.

"I'll bring you to *rot*, Lucas," Clyde fumed. The withered hand made a fist, and dust from the spirit's own skin crumpled to the ground. "You'll rot for eternity!"

At his words, the ground began to shake. A cloud suddenly passed over the sun, making the streets below sweep away in darkness. I took a step back, terrified. Had dead Clyde become more powerful than living Clyde? How was that possible?

As if reading my mind, I felt a hand on my shoulder. Rowley pulled me back gently, a worried look on his face.

"It's not for you."

"You're coming down with me," Clyde yelled, and I finally understood what he meant. Clyde lunged at me, fury in his eyes when something grabbed him from the air.

A void ripped open from the ground. A jagged strip broke the cement in two as an inky black figure rose to the earth. The creature struggled through with gnarled, clawed hands. Steam wafted from its open sores, as if it had been burned. It resembled a skeleton, or something tortured enough to look like one. Its cry was one between a child's shriek and a victim's scream. It hooked onto Clyde, stopping him from assault. Clyde fought back, and almost looked successful until another clamped onto him. And another. And soon a whole hoard of creatures were tugging and fighting with Clyde, suffocating and killing him. Their fingers were like acid on his skin, which seemed to peel at their slightest touch. And then there was the scream. I can't even begin to describe the scream.

The victim, the thing, surrounded by skulls, clambered forward, using all means possible to stay out of the void. Inch by inch, despite his frantic attempts, he was losing. The frantic soul was sinking farther and farther into the pit. A hand managed to grab the edge, the sound of his gasps choking and withering.

I almost felt bad. I thought about stepping forward to help, but Rowley's hand was gripped onto my shoulder, holding me back. There was no way I could stop this. It had been decided. Clyde was beyond what either of us could do.

The struggle was almost over. Three bloody fingers slipped from his grip, and Clyde lost his battle with death. He sank into the pit, the demons piling to push him in farther. As quick as it happened, the portal closed up, the cloud left the sun, and the world was right again.

"That," Rowley told me, "is what happens to the bad people." My core felt choked and dry. I gave a silent nod. I understood now.

For two-hundred years Clyde Harrison had owed the Devil. And as I stared at the healed sidewalk, it was clear. His debt had been paid.

Chapter 46

When someone dies, there is usually a moment of silence to honor them. And sometimes there's a moment of silence even when the person who died wasn't like in the first place. It just sort of happens. When somebody dies the way Clyde did, it takes your breath away even when you don't have any. It's something that needs a moment of silence, something you have to remember together. Completely still, the two of us had a period where we didn't say a word. No matter who you are, that kind of death is a tragedy.

So in that moment, we watched the spot where it had all happened. Clyde's body was still there, but it didn't seem that important anymore.

A siren sounded in the distance. "He's gone man," Rowley said. I nodded, and we said nothing more. That was all that needed to be said.

"Rowley! Lucas!" Cleo cried, racing down the street to us. We turned to find her, Sarah, and Rico heading toward us, relived looks on their faces. None of them had seen the body.

"I'm not sure this is the best place for a reunion," Rowley half smiled, darting over to the group. "You guys might wanna move."

"Clyde's dead," Cleo said, looking at me earnestly. "We know."

I came to stand by Rowley. "You felt it?"

"No." Despite the fact someone had died, Sarah smiled in relief. "I did."

She jumped forward and hugged me. This time I was smart enough to hug her back. I closed my eyes and couldn't help but smile. Despite everything that had happened, it felt good to be with the others again.

"I'm glad you're ok," she breathed when we let go. I looked at her, sweating, out of breath. She looked so alive. The barrier between us was only going to grow larger.

"Me too," I smiled back.

"Actually, I didn't pick up on the whole psychic-knowing thing. What happened?" Rico asked.

"We got into a little scuff," Rowley explained. "He and Alder won't be making any more deals."

"Yeah," I said, the thought sinking in. Rowley had abandoned his last connection to the living. "What about your brother?"

I don't think Rowley was expecting that question. He thought for a moment.

"I think," Rowley paused, as if not sure how to put it into words. "I think he knows I'll be all right. I think he always has. But if I could, I'd tell him I was here."

"And always will be?" I finished, poking fun.

"Nah." Rowley looked at me. "I think you know."

I did. I felt it since Clyde had died, but I wasn't sure. I didn't know if I could leave, but I don't think it was my choice. It was beyond my control.

There was still one matter to attend to. "What happened to the knife?" Sarah asked. "We need to find it before someone else does."

"I have it here, actually," I explained. My hand came out of my pocket to reveal the knife, still polished and perfect in form. It seemed even after years of use nothing could tarnish the blade. That in itself was reason to cause alarm.

"I'll take it," Sarah offered. "It's best we keep watch over it until we figure out how to get rid of it."

Nodding in agreement I handed it over. Somehow, I knew I wouldn't be around to see the knife destroyed. The living would have to figure it out, and I trusted them to handle it. I turned toward the sun, the bright sky. All these things here— earth— all these living things were something I didn't belong to anymore.

I paused for a moment, not sure what to say. "Guys?"

"We know," Sarah smiled, a tear forming in her eye. "It's time."

But it didn't feel that way. Something inside me told me there was one more part of my calling, one last reason to stay.

"Actually," I said, smiling to myself, "there's one more thing I have to do."

~

I stood outside the apartment, knowing with total confidence where I was. A small part of me leaped in recognition when I saw the building. I smiled to myself, taking Sarah's hand.

"Welcome home," I said to myself as I walked up the steps. The door would be locked; the complex always locked its doors. Fortunately for me, there was a spare set of keys still inside a statue by the door. Rico got it for me and unlocked the door. The click was music to my ears.

"Apartment 2B," I instructed, heading up the stairs ahead of the others.

"We've been to your house before," Rico pointed out, following. Sarah elbowed him.

"Nice place," Rowley smiled. He floated up to my side. "Who are we visiting?"

I didn't hide my smile. "My family. My only family."

"Right, dead parents," he reminded himself. "But who?"

I stopped at the door. Slowly, hesitantly, Sarah's hand came up in the shape of a fist. It felt right in that moment. I knew, I just knew I was supposed to do it.

We knocked on the door.

"Coming, coming," the familiar voice sounded, along with the shuffling across the floor. Walking was hard for her recently. The others made it to my side with time to spare.

"But DG," Cleo asked. "Can she see you?"

The door opened. A woman, one with my green eyes and my father's smile, stood on the other side of the door, looking up at us in confusion. She was an old woman, slightly hunched with her withered hands that were prone to quiver. Her silver hair was tied in a bun, but a few locks managed to spill out onto her shoulders. She was the shortest among us, beating Cleo by a few inches. The five of us stood there, not knowing what to say. Suddenly, my grandma burst into a smile.

"Lucas!"

Chapter 47

She insisted that we sit with her, though Rowley had refused. It took her a while to make her way across the apartment, but she showed us to the living room and managed to make the live ones some drinks. The entire time we explained what had happened, each of us chiming in with our sides of the story and other details. I stayed by her side the whole time, making sure she didn't drop anything and that she was ok.

"I waited a whole *week* for this young man to come home," she was telling the group while setting her teacup on the table. "And he was a no-show. You really made your grandma start to worry!"

"It feels like I was the only one that was concerned by the fact I was dead," I noticed, sitting on the couch.

"You know your father's gift didn't come out of nowhere," my grandma reminded me. There was a spark in her eye whenever she looked at me. I could help but smile when she looked at me like that. "It was awfully lonely here without you."

My eyes fell to the ground, the small smile on my face fading. "I'm sorry."

She gave me a stern look, one I'd seen several times in my life. "Lucas." I looked at her. "Don't ever feel sorry for being dead," she scolded me. "And don't worry that you beat me to it. I won't hold it over you."

I looked away, smiling. Somehow I knew that coming back here was what I had been searching for this whole time.

"Your grandson has completed your son's work," Cleo explained. "I'm sure your family's spirits can rest easy now."

"Oh, there will always be restless spirits," she said to Cleo. "That's what we're here for." She looked over to Sarah. "Am I right?"

Sarah met eyes with my grandmother, finally understanding. She got up, walking over to Rowley.

"My sister is Maddie Conwell," Sarah explained, looking up at him. "And I'm Sarah Conwell. We used to live across the street from each other. You probably don't remember me."

"What? No way!" Rowley interrupted, his eyes lighting up. He took Sarah's hands, and she smiled at him. "Little Connie? From when you were like, five?"

I remembered the girl from Rowley's memories. Connie, *Conwell*. It was a nickname.

Sarah laughed at the memory. "Um, yeah."

"I totally remember you now," Rowley exclaimed, floating around excitedly. "We never hung out 'cause you were a crybaby," he stopped, rethinking what he said. "No offense."

Sarah shrugged it off. "It's fine."

"There's so much I need to say," Rowley realized, stopping where he was. "Will, Maddie, Tristan— you should probably write this all down."

He went off talking, and from the looks of it he wouldn't be done for a while. I smiled to myself, glad Rowley could finally do what he'd wanted to do twelve years ago. I turned to my grandma.

"How'd you know?"

She laughed. "Her gift was strongest around you. I knew you'd lead her to something."

I agreed. From observing them Rowley didn't seem like he'd stop talking anytime soon. Sarah listened, overwhelmed but content. Even without me her gift would have a good use.

"Two kids meeting up like that," she smiled, years of experience gleaming in her eyes. "There had to be something divine involved."

Cleo was making small talk with Rico, who was nodding and adding in intently. I could see that even with me gone life would go on for the living. And just maybe, it would turn out ok.

"Lucas?"

I turned to my grandma. She was peering up at me, a sad look in her grey green eyes that had been rare in my lifetime. She knew, and I knew. It was easier this way, not having to explain it. I could feel it in my heart of hearts that our time had come. She smiled at me.

"Go home."

I needed to hear those words, I think. Like Rowley, I really couldn't have gone without her telling me to. Her words were the final blessing for both of us, the password to passing on. Maybe I wasn't after avenging my father or getting back at Alder. Maybe after this whole time, I just wanted to say goodbye.

Rico interrupted my thoughts. He had stopped talking to Cleo and looked up, astounded. "Um, Lucas?"

There wasn't any need to correct him. Rico wasn't facing the wrong way this time. He was looking at me, right at me.

Chapter 48

He was looking at me, I mean straight at me. Rico's lack of sight didn't matter anymore. His eyes met mine for the first time since I had died, and some kind of exchange passed between us.

I blinked. "Rico?"

He blinked. "Lucas?" He shook his head, still looking at me, "Oh my gosh man!" he cried, running forward and throwing him arms at me. There wasn't any point in being embarrassed about it in front of family. Nothing like that was on our minds. I accepted it, my eyes still wide and confused. He could see me? He could touch me? What was this? "Dude, you still look so much like— you."

We let go, and I managed a smile. "I still am."

I looked over at my grandma, not knowing what to say to say. She smiled at me and nodded, knowing too there was nothing left to say.

"Go on," she told me.

Cleo stood up. She didn't need her sixth sense to know what was going on.

"Think of me," she said to Rowley and me, her calm voice something close to something sad, "and I'll think of you."

We nodded. Where we went next, even a psychic couldn't follow.

Lastly I turned to Sarah. She had wiped something off her face, but only laughed when I caught her.

"Just go," she smiled, turning away. "I'll be all right."

I threw my arms around her, so fast it almost caught her off guard. She stumbled back, almost not knowing what to do. She placed her arms around me, closing her eyes with a small smile on her face.

"I love you," I said. "Remember that."

She took in a breath, a living, beautiful breath I would miss forever. "I always will."

"DG," Rowley whispered, drifting closer to us while keeping his distance. "I hate to interrupt, but—"

"Yeah," I smiled, letting go. "I know."

I turned, already knowing what would be behind me. It had appeared through the roof of the apartment, gleaming so bright it was like the ceiling wasn't there. It was a white light— kind of cliché, but you knew it was there. It always was.

"Nice meeting y'all," Rowley waved. He pointed at Sarah. "Don't forget!"

"Never," she grinned.

"*Auf Weidersehen!* See you next fall! Later gator. Don't screw up the planet while we're gone!"

I followed Rowley, who drifted farther and farther up into the sky. I stepped up, and a set of stairs appeared at my feet. Soon afterward a rail came to aid my hand. We were going up, passing on, finally taking our last steps on earth.

"Bye dude!" Rico waved, looking clearly at Rowley for the first and last time.

"Fair well!" Cleo chimed in.

"Bye!" Sarah waved, craning to see me as I climbed higher and higher into the air.

I smiled at them, no words coming to my mouth. For the first time, despite leaving, despite what had happened, despite everything horrible that had ever happened in my life— I felt ok.

"*Saiyounara*! Bye bye! *Aidios*!" Rowley called, passed me and practically in the light. I had slowed to look at them one last time, when Rowley grabbed my hood. "Come *on* DG!"

I turned, looking beyond the earth to the landscape that lay before me. I had never really thought about what "the beyond" would look like, or imagined myself in it. But the place I was looking at, this place I was in far surpassed anything I had ever pictured in my life. I stepped off the staircase onto the grass, and I knew at that moment I was home.

I would always miss my friends, my family, and my life. But I knew it would be ok. I would see them again.

ABOUT THE AUTHOR

Abby Schnell is a freshman at Grand Valley State University. She grew up with a thousand stuffed animals and an intense desire to tell stories. When she was five, she acted out her ideas with her toys. At age eight she used interpretative dance. By the time she turned eighteen she learned how to communicate through the written word. Now Abby hopes to use these story-telling skills as a writer. She aspires to find work after graduation as an editor, screenwriter, or anywhere in between.

Made in the USA
Lexington, KY
27 September 2015